I0630694

ROYALLY SCREWED

PACIFIC PASSIONS - BOOK ONE

COURTNEY CLARK MICHAELS

AUGUST PUBLISHING

CONTENT NOTES

This book contains depiction of the following: unplanned pregnancy due to birth control failure, parents who have passed prior to the book, a minor character with a gambling addiction, nonconsensual recording of a character during intimate moments (off-page, historical), and a car accident injuring a secondary character (off-page, historic). Every effort has been taken by the author to handle these with sensitivity, however please consider whether this content may impact you as a reader, and take care of yourself.

For Mum who gave me books, and Dad who gave me speeches.

GLOSSARY

Fafine aulelei – beautiful woman
Palagi – foreigner
Malo – Hello (informal)
Leai – No
Whangai – adoption or fostering of a child by family members
Pepe – baby
Tapa – beaten barkcloth used as fabric
Loto'a – inside the fence.
Fale – house
Talitane – whore
O outou o 'au – You are mine.
Mana – spiritual power, authority or influence
Panipopo – coconut buns
Taualuga – traditional Polynesian dance
Chee hoo – a colloquial expression of excitement. Can be used for celebration or as a challenge.
Fa'afafine – the recognized third gender in Samoa, individuals who are born with male genitalia but identify and are raised as women, either fully or in part.
Puletasi – a traditional style of modest two-piece dress worn in the Pacific Islands.
O la'u ia – She is mine.
Lavalava – a traditional item of clothing worn by men and women in the Pacific Islands, similar to a wraparound skirt or a sarong.
Tagaloa – the supreme ruler or chief of all gods in Samoan mythology.

ONE

A lush wall of frangipani rose up the side of the villa's balcony, its tropical scent wafting through the air to mix with the heady aroma of salt, sand and serenity. The stunning two-story Spanish-inspired building overlooking its own white sand lagoon on the South Pacific island of Avali might as well have been plucked from an encyclopedia entry entitled 'Paradise'.

"Are you freaking *kidding* me?"

Frustration sent Stella Warren's voice slicing through the tranquil setting like a razor blade, as she raised her smartphone higher in the air in the hope that its proximity to God might help answer her prayers.

"How can I run a wedding without phone reception?"

Since no answer was forthcoming from either the Almighty or the frangipani-scented breeze, she huffed out a sigh and turned towards the villa's ornately carved front door.

To-do list. Find a spot with reception. Check wifi capabilities. Ask about a landline for the villa.

As she rattled off the list in her head, Stella felt her breath even out.

As long as there's a plan.

Her detail-oriented nature had made her one of New Zealand's most sought-after wedding planners, but it also meant she did not do well with unexpected complications. And the possibility of relying on a landline and dial-up Internet to pull together her best friend's wedding in a remote corner of the South Pacific was most definitely an unexpected complication.

She stabbed at the doorbell placed discreetly to the side of the villa's entrance with a perfectly manicured finger as the list in her head continued.

Update the run sheet with the new communications details. Get in touch with the florist asap. Check with -

Stella broke off mid-thought as the door swung open and she found herself swimming in the smoky eyes of a tall, dark disaster.

No.

Framed in the doorway like the sexiest portrait ever painted stood the single biggest mistake of her life. Prince Aleki Esera of Avali had swanned into her life at eighteen, and left her heartbroken ten months later.

"Stella?"

His utterance of her name hit her ears at the same time the breath left her body. Shock flooded Stella's system, rising in her throat like a tidal wave, coating her tongue in a bitter residue as memories bombarded her in rapid fire succession.

"What are you *doing* here?"

Aleki winced, crinkles bracketing his chocolate-coloured eyes in a way she hadn't seen before. A very, very good way.

"A little more high-pitched, thanks. I'm not sure every dog on the island heard you."

"You're the only dog on this island, Aleki Esera," Stella snapped, heat rising in her cheeks. Even now, shame and regret pounding a dual beat through her body in time with her racing heart, she couldn't stem the shiver of awareness that trickled down her spine at the sight of him.

The bronze skin that had so attracted her attention during their university days in Wellington shone with a burnished glow that spoke volumes of his life on the island since he'd left New Zealand's vibrant capital. His features had sharpened, strong eyebrows and a square jaw caging the richness of his eyes and full lips that would have made Michelangelo weep. The pull of a faded olive t-shirt over the broad expanse of his chest hinted at a physique more aligned with an Olympic athlete than a pampered prince who in her memories had exerted more energy in bars and bedrooms than in gyms.

Even as her consciousness fought against the sultry hum of her blood, appreciation slid through her body, warming her insides.

Aleki had always exerted an otherworldly pull on her. Ever since the first time she'd laid eyes on him tossing a rugby ball around on the field under the cable car stop, she'd been hooked. It was the raw magnetism that throbbed between them when they were together, tangible as a neon light, that had led to her inevitable undoing and the resulting debacle that had coloured Stella's dating life since.

Seemingly unperturbed by the riot of emotions barraging her, Aleki simply folded his lean six-two frame over to clasp a strong, tanned hand around the handle of her monogrammed suitcase.

"Are you coming in?"

"Are you crazy? Why are you even here? This is a private residence. You need to leave, now!"

Even as she looked wildly around for the sleek black sedan that had collected her from the airport and dropped her in this surreal situation, Aleki's deep chuckle wrapped around her, his amusement deepening her panic rather than lightening the mood.

"The car is gone, Stella. And since it is my car, and my driver, it was unlikely to take me anywhere I didn't wish to go. Today is a day for staying home, I think."

Home.

The word reverberated through Stella like a gong, sealing her fate as the realisation sunk in, settling heavily in her stomach.

"This is your house." She forced the words out in as flat a tone as she could manage, even as her emotions swirled inside her like a maelstrom.

What is Mae thinking?

Since the engagement, Stella's jewellery designer best friend had talked of little else than holding her wedding on the tropical island of Avali, renowned for crystal clear waters popular with divers the world over and its' impressive reef conservation efforts.

Having seen the way the abundant forestry hugged the powdered-sugar shoreline along the island's coast and the lively bustle of Havalei'i, the island's single steel-and-glass city often referred to as 'Honolulu of the South', Stella could well understand her friend's desire to cement her romance in such a stunning setting.

Any resistance that might have tugged low in her gut about her history with the island nation's heir had been assuaged by repeated assurances from her brain that running into him by chance was an impossibility, and from various women's magazines that he was in fact busy running into Victoria's Secret models in Iceland.

But for Mae to host her wedding *here*? In his *home*? And no doubt *invite* him?

"Who is Lani? Every email I've received about this event has been signed by her."

"My assistant. She handles the administrative details of my home."

"And Mae knew this whole time?"

Aleki's firm mouth lifted at one corner.

"We wanted it to be a surprise. A fun little reunion."

You must be kidding.

She couldn't blame her best friend. Stella had never told Mae about Aleki's final evening in New Zealand. About the night that the pool of desire that had simmered in her blood since meeting him had finally fizzed to the surface, only to be met with equal passion from the prince. Nor had she mentioned the way his hands had blazed across her skin, setting fire to her synapses, her familiarity with the rasp of his stubble across her sensitive skin or the lust-soaked kisses that drugged her into a state of near spiritual bliss.

She most certainly had never mentioned that she'd awoken to cold bedsheets and the news that her royal lover had taken leave of the country mere hours after she'd taken leave of her senses and offered him everything she had.

Even now, that memory, coupled with the long, lazy examination Aleki was subjecting her to was enough to send lustful sparks shooting through her abdomen.

And he arranged for me to be here. Without a heads up, without a chance to back out.

That realization was enough to bring Stella to her senses.

She was no longer a naive virgin, and he was no longer the man she'd spent hours talking and laughing with in the university library, a fact she was sure several of the world's finest lingerie models could attest to.

Stella Warren was the epitome of professionalism. She was a colour-coding, flower-girl-wrangling, mother-minimizing, wedding-planning perfectionist. And after seven years in the industry, she was damn good at it. Facing a former lover at a destination wedding barely registered in her personal folio of acceptable freak-out circumstances. Red wine on a couture wedding dress? *That* was a problem. This was merely an annoyance. And she would not allow a simple annoyance to ruin Mae's wedding. Especially not one that had been in her pants.

WATCHING her as closely as he was, Aleki saw the exact moment Stella gave into her sense of duty. Her shoulders rose just a little, her back straightened, and emerald fire flashed in the depths of her eyes.

Fighting eyes, he'd called them in the past when they shone that way. She didn't let them out often - his Stella was too reserved for that - but every now and then when faced with injustice they would shine, and he would stand back and watch in awe while she took on fights bigger than herself. The disability discrimination in the university's swim team, the reduced funding to the arts faculty, the campaign for gender neutral bathrooms - the eighteen-year-old Stella who had captivated him so during his year of study abroad had no problems fighting for a noble cause.

Clearly she had come to the conclusion that Mae's

wedding was too worthy an event to risk ruining with her obvious distaste for her host.

Lucky for him.

His eyes lingered over her in a perusal that catalogued every change in her face and body since he'd left her slumbering in his Wellington apartment ten years ago.

Shame from how he'd handled the sudden call from his father demanding his return to the island still lapped at him, yet still his gaze slid hungrily over her creamy skin, set off perfectly by the stark black of her scoop neck tank dress. Lush waves of caramel and chocolate coloured tresses framed her cheeks, their blunt ends brushing against the top of her collarbones.

Desire tugged in his gut as he let his gaze travel down, to the rich curve of her breast, the sensual sweep of her hip flaring out from her waist, pausing at last as he reached his final destination, the anticipation gnawing at his senses as he reached her legs.

Miles long, lightly tanned and well-shaped, Stella's legs had made both her first and final impression on him. The last time he'd been this close to those legs, he'd been untangling his own from them and sliding out from the cotton sheets tangled around their naked bodies to grab his phone before the vibration's low murmur against his oak bedside table woke her.

Regret had flowed through his system as he'd dressed quietly in the dark and departed in the wake of his father's call. Even now it left a sour tang in the back of his throat as he drank in the sight of Stella on his doorstep.

Here. For a week.

He loved Mae and her fiancé Luke, who'd been his first friend in New Zealand, but he'd be lying to himself if he didn't admit that the chance to see Stella again had factored into his eagerness to provide his estate for the happy couple's nuptials.

"Come in," he offered, stepping back and dragging her case across the threshold and onto the wide terracotta tiles of his foyer.

She followed it through the doorway, although a slight hesitation at the threshold belied her reluctance. Aleki watched as her expressive green eyes darted up towards the high white ceilings, intercut with exposed dark wooden rafters, and to the black wrought iron staircase with its Pacifica mosaic design that meandered up and around to the ornate internal balustrade that seperated the second level of bedrooms and bathrooms from the living areas below.

A tight tangle of nervous energy pressed against Aleki's chest from the inside as Stella took in her luxurious surroundings. Although he had a right to rooms in the royal estate currently occupied by his father, Aleki had chosen to build his own home on a private corner of the island, a haven from the politics of palace life and the photographers from international tabloids that still flocked to Avali in the warmer months to try and snap a picture of him in various states of undress.

I hope she likes it.

The thought sprang unbidden into his consciousness as Stella took further inventory of her surroundings.

"How many power points are in this area?"

Aleki's anxiety around Stella's opinion of his home vanished in the wake of her practical question.

Of course.

While he'd been hoping for a sign of her approval, she'd been cataloguing his electrical capacity.

He deserved no more.

"I'm not sure." Apology coloured his voice. "You'd need to check with Lani, or with maintenance."

For a private residence, Aleki's home swarmed with too many damn people in his opinion. Every week he waited longingly for Sunday, the day of rest for the people of Avali, when a skeleton security staff monitored the perimeter leaving him blissfully undisturbed for one precious day.

"I'd like to see the papaya grove. Mae is hoping we can use it for the pre-wedding picnic and lawn games the day before the service."

Seizing the opportunity, Aleki's voice sprung forth before he could stop it.

"Connect Four?"

Stella's eyes narrowed, emerald sparks flaring to life in her irises she made eye contact with him for the first time since entering the house.

"*Not* Connect Four."

A flirtatious grin tugged at the corner of Aleki's mouth.

"We always had a good time playing Connect Four, Stella."

If looks could kill, he would be vapourised into small enough particles that Mae and Luke could use him as confetti during the ceremony. But not even the ferocity in Stella's gaze was enough for him to ignore the memories of their last game of Connect Four that flooded through him. An epic battle of strategy, skill, and finally, with the pieces scattered across the bed like plastic rose petals, seduction. His blood stirred just remembering it.

"I'm sure we can find other activities to amuse you on the day, Your Highness." Stella's tone could have flash-frozen a bonfire. "After all, you're such a very good player."

Aleki's dark gaze grew serious and he sought to capture her eyes so that she might be assured of his sincerity.

"I never played with you, Stella."

"Of course not," she responded flippantly. "'Play' implies a game. A game implies rules. You just took what you wanted and left."

Hollowness ballooned in Aleki's stomach. There it was, out in the open. And judging by Stella's inflection and the ice in her eyes, she was in no mood to forgive or forget. Lowering his gaze, he did the only thing he could in the situation. A delicate withdrawal. There would be time later to convince her of his remorse. She was staying under his roof for a week, after all.

"I'll show you to your bedroom. I'm sure you would find a nap beneficial."

"Why? Do you have a flight to catch?"

Her barb hit home, the sardonic tone of her question contrasting with her saccharine smile fueling the fire of regret that still simmered low in his gut.

You never should have left her that way.

Aleki shook his head slightly to clear the chiding voice that had popped up to remind him of his cowardice in leaving Stella from time to time over the last decade. Since Mae had informed him Stella would not only be attending her wedding but arriving a week before the date to coordinate the event, that voice had been as persistent and unwelcome as the mosquitos that haunted the rainforest to the north of the island.

He had been young and frightened of the strength of his feelings for the beautiful brunette, not just the lust she inspired in him, but of how happy he was just sitting and talking with her. Even at eighteen, Stella Warren was a woman who made a man think dangerous thoughts – like commitment. Love. Forever.

Aleki had been burned by those thoughts before and

the embers of distrust still smouldered in his heart. When King Tama had called in the milky hours of morning telling him to return home, he'd grabbed at the royal summons like a liferaft. If anything, his father's voice had pulled him back from the messy brink of emotion faster than anything else could have. After Aleki's mother's death when he was three, the king had barely smiled. His entire focus was the kingdom. As Aleki's should have been. But with Stella...

The playboy lifestyle he'd thrown himself into after leaving Stella's slumbering frame had done nothing to stem his fascination with her. He was older now, and wiser. Wise enough to know that women like Stella were rare, and he wanted more than one night to lose himself in her.

Stella Warren was about to learn that Prince Aleki always got what he wanted.

TWO

The morning sun spilled onto the patio, dazzling in the saturated blue of the sky. Stella scooped up another silky spoonful of her satsuma and coconut chia cup, luxuriating in the peace and beauty of her surroundings. For someone who spent hours out of each day dashing around checking items off a never-ending list, breakfast had become her sacred time. Half an hour to herself, with a cup of English Breakfast tea and a soundtrack of birdsong never failed to put her at ease prior to the chaos of her days.

Today's birdsong was live, courtesy of a variety of the island's birds that darted through the boxed garden adjacent to the terracotta tiled patio and pool area. Their unfamiliar chorus swirled around her as she leaned back in the deep cushion of her patio chair, closed her eyes and drew in a cleansing breath of tropical air. In twenty minutes she would turn on her phone, connect to the Internet using the wifi code left on her bedside table last night in the bold slashes of Aleki's handwriting, and her day would officially begin. But for now, peace and quiet.

"Good morning."

The deep, masculine rumble of a certain royal's voice pierced the stillness, sending tension thrumming through her body and a tingle through her core.

Shifting slightly in her chair in a futile attempt to alleviate the sudden throb of awareness at the centre of her, Stella cracked one eye open.

Aleki stood above her, clothed in a white shirt and tailored grey pants and holding a steaming mug, looking every inch the urbane royal. The easy contentment of her breakfast gone, Stella felt the crackle of unwanted attraction snapping at her when he sank into the chair opposite. The rich aroma of coffee danced across the table to Stella, the intensity of the scent a perfect metaphor for the man himself, turning her inside out just by the dark look he levelled at her from his seat opposite.

Taken aback by the rush of hormones flitting through her bloodstream like a swarm of Ritalin-deprived butterflies, Stella dropped her eyes to her breakfast.

In and out. In and out.

The mantra echoed in her head as she concentrated on breathing like a proper grown up rather than melting into an inelegant blob of desire at Aleki's Italian-shod feet.

"I thought you'd be busy. Or eat in the house. Or be anywhere else other than out here with me."

"Ah, Stella," Aleki chided gently in his melodic accent, "what kind of host would I be to leave you to your own devices so early in your stay? Besides, I've yet to show you the papaya grove. You'll like it. Plenty of space for games."

"I don't need hosting. I need to pick up a thirty metre extension cord and fifty citronella candles. Feel free to go reign - or to *play* - while I'm here."

Aleki's dark eyes roamed over her, his interest no less focused in the wake of her snarky tone. Her skin prickled as the flesh left bare by her cream linen shorts and strappy black tank heated and flushed. The hot depths of his gaze remained on her even while he moved back in his seat to allow an unobtrusive staff member to set a plate piled high with steaming food in front of him. The smell of bacon and French toast teased her nostrils, and she stared down at her own breakfast with a firm mental reminder that early morning fibre was her friend.

"Look at me, Stella." His deep voice pulled her focus from her fresh fruit platter as she reluctantly raised her gaze to meet his. Dark eyes assessed her thoroughly, skating over her pale skin like a caress.

"You are my guest and my friend. We may not have seen each other in the last ten years, but I have fond memories of all of the time that we spent together in New Zealand, and it is my pleasure to have you here in Avali. You were kind enough to show me around your country when I lived there. It would be my honour if you would allow me to do the same while you are here on the island."

Some of the tension pinching at Stella's shoulders eased. He was right. Despite the wash of shame that still flooded her when she thought about that night, she had considered Aleki one of her best friends, and he had been nothing but a gracious host so far even in the face of her hostility. The best thing for everyone, especially Mae and Luke, would be to accept his kind offer and enjoy her time here with him, friends again.

Even as the thought crossed her mind, her eyes met his and a zing of awareness frissoned through her, tightening her nipples and catching her breath at the back of her throat.

Oh yeah, Stella. Just relegate the hottest guy you've ever met back into the friend-zone. No worries.

Electricity zipped through her body as a knowing half-smile hitched one side of Aleki's full mouth, flashing her an endearing dimple.

With a supreme effort usually reserved for declining dessert during business lunches, Stella wrenched her thoughts back from what Aleki's perfect mouth could do to her and tried to focus on what it - *he* - had just said.

"Fine. If it isn't an inconvenience to you, I would love to see the papaya grove. But I do have a meeting with a supplier at eleven in the city so it will need to be shortly."

Fighting off the vestiges of attraction made her voice brisker than usual, but Aleki didn't seem to notice her staccato delivery.

"Perfect. We'll walk down to the grove after breakfast, and I can accompany you to Havalei'i afterwards. I have some business to attend to myself, and it would be wasteful for us to make two trips when we can easily travel together."

Seemingly satisfied with the matter, he dug into his food while Stella tried to figure out how he'd managed to charm her from civility to companionship without her noticing.

In and out. In and out.

"So fifty citronella candles, huh?" Aleki eyed her, scooping up another forkful of pancakes. "That's a lot of firepower for a few little bugs."

"You have no idea," Stella assured him. "One of my first weddings when I started out working as an assistant for this huge event planning company was in the Marlborough Sounds. The couple were a soap actress and her investment banker fiancé. It cost an obscene amount of money - a Michelin star chef, individual hand-poured candles in the couples' signature scent for favours, fireworks at midnight - the whole nine yards. But nobody thought about the mosquitos. It was a disaster. Every person present was eaten alive. Embossed menus that cost thirty dollars a pop were being used for swatters, the servers were snapping napkins all over the place, the bride was crying and the groom offered a thousand dollar reward for anyone who could provide her with insect repellent. Since then, every single outdoor event I've planned has included a budget for citronella candles."

"You were part of a disastrous event? I don't believe it." Aleki declared.

She lifted her cup of tea to her lips and smirked.

"As a lowly assistant in a chain of experts the buck stopped miles from me. But I took my thousand dollar reward from that night and invested it. That money was the first chunk of savings towards going out on my own."

A low, deep chuckle full of admiration drifted across the table.

"Insect repellent?"

"A girl can never be too prepared."

Aleki shook his head slightly.

"You are something else, Stella Warren."

Warmth settled in her chest at his praise, a soft enveloping glow that pulsed gently outwards.

Desperate to break the cocoon of intimacy that had settled over the patio table, Stella's gaze settled on Aleki's breakfast.

"How can you eat all of that?"

Aleki lifted a shoulder.

"Being the heir to the throne of a country is hard work. Carbo-loading is essential," he joked.

"There's three normal breakfasts on that plate. That's not carbo-loading, it's a fast-track to diabetes."

"Lani spoils me when I'm home. Besides-" Aleki leaned back in his chair and patted his taut abdomen. "-I run."

An indelicate snort escaped Stella before she could stop it.

"Chasing tail isn't exactly on the approved-cardio list."

"And yet it keeps my heart unquestionably safe," Aleki smirked, sending her a playful wink.

Stella's breath caught in her chest at his flirtatious tone. Desire cracked across the air between them as his hot, dark eyes locked on hers, sweeping away her controlled demeanor in a tide of rising heat. A slideshow of memories flashed through her mind as the moment rolled on - the rough burr of his furred chest against her cheek, her fingers locked in the thick, silky strands of his hair, the thrilling graze of his teeth against the tender skin of her neck.

Eyes blazing, Aleki half-stood from the table, one dark hand reaching for her. Cupping her cheek, his gaze bore through her, razing her good intentions to ashes in its wake.

"If you want to achieve anything today, you should leave the table now, *fafine aulelei*" he rasped. "Otherwise, the only place I'll be escorting you is my bedroom."

Lust throbbed deep in Stella's core, reverberating outwards. Her nipples pebbled beneath her tank top, straining towards Aleki like a magnetic force. The hitch of her breath sawed through the still morning air. Nothing, nobody, had ever affected her like Aleki Esera.

"My Stella." The soft words hung between them, guiding the path as Aleki moved forward, his eyes fixed on her lips.

That small motion was all it took to break the spell.

No, no, no, no, no!

Passion turned to panic, swirling through Stella like a tropical hurricane. She stumbled backwards, out of Aleki's reach as her mind whirred.

This is what he does. He makes you feel special, but you're not.

The blazing certainty cut through her like a knife, hot and hard. She had been burnt before, but not this time. Not again.

Avoiding his gaze, Stella did the only thing she could think of under the circumstances. She ran.

SILENCE HUNG in the back of the limo as the car slid smoothly along the coastal highway towards the city. Stella worked on her laptop, connected to the vehicle's wifi, while Aleki took the time to answer emails and confirm his schedule for the following week with his secretary. Following the wedding he was expected to travel to Samoa to finalize a trade agreement. Try though he might to focus on the details of the trip, economic forecasts and tax law couldn't complete with the intoxicating fragrance of Stella's perfume drifting over to him. Aleki inhaled, and the back of the luxury car seemed to shrink as her scent teased his nostrils.

Following his declaration at the breakfast table, her eyes had widened in a way that would have been comical, had he not been so aroused, and she had bolted like the hounds of hell were nipping at her heels. While some men might take offense at the object of their desire beating such a hasty departure, Aleki was not one of them. His Stella did not shy away from confrontation, so any escape on her part was avoidance rather than agitation. Triumph swelled in his chest.

She feels it, too.

Stella shifted in her seat again, tucking a strand of

golden brown hair behind her ear and sending another whiff of her fresh, clean scent towards him.

Awareness buzzed under Aleki's skin, tightening his stomach and giving way to the low throb of desire in his blood. Huffing out an exhalation, he gave up all pretense of work and turned towards the source of his distraction.

"What are you wearing?"

Stella cut her green eyes from her laptop screen to him, peering up at him from under a lush fringe of lashes. A familiar lust wrapped itself around him like an old blanket.

"Shorts?" Wariness edged her response. "Is that not okay? The Avali tourism website said that modest dress was encouraged but not enforced. They're not *short* shorts."

Truthfully, the only notice Aleki had taken of her shorts were that they emphasized the toned length of her legs. She'd slipped on a pair of tan sandals before leaving the villa and their toffee colour only served to make it appear that her legs went on forever. A fact Aleki was most appreciative of.

"Not your outfit." He waved a hand dismissively, batting her uncertainty over her clothing choices away. "Your perfume. What is it?"

Stella cocked one dark, perfectly sculpted eyebrow and openly assessed him.

"It's Green Tea, by Elizabeth Arden," she admitted, after a short pause.

"It's beautiful."

Now she was looking at him like he was crazy.

"It's like, forty bucks, dude."

"Dude?"

"We're friends. Friends call each other 'dude'."

Dismissing her use of the least-romantic endearment in the history of time, Aleki persisted.

"I'm serious. It smells..." He paused, searching for the right word. "Refreshing. It's not too flowery, too sweet. It's crisp and light. Why do you wear that one?"

"My mother wore it." She spoke so softly he had to strain to hear it, even in the quiet of the car.

"Ah."

The silence permeated through the still interior, heavy and dark.

"I was sorry to hear of her passing." Aleki uttered gently.

Stella offered him a small smile.

"Thank you."

"I thought about sending flowers, but I didn't know if you wanted to hear from me. It seemed a bit trite, given the circumstances. I made a contribution to the Wellington Library in her name instead."

Her eyes widened slightly and a rosy flush crept across her cheeks.

"That's very kind of you. It wasn't necessary, but she would have appreciated the gesture."

"And your father? Do you still see him?"

"Not if I can help it." The softness that had cushioned her voice evaporated, a steel edge cutting through her New Zealand accent instead, deepening her vowels while a crease marred her forehead.

Aleki had only a rudimentary knowledge of Stella's relationship with her father, gleaned mostly from Luke and from the few curt remarks Stella had made about him during their university days.

Like how if she wanted to see him at graduation she'd need to hold her celebratory dinner at a dog track. He still remembered the way she'd looked saying that, the sun streaming in through the library window, picking out strands of gold in her hair and the lettering of the dusty old commerce textbooks stacked in a haphazard pile on the table between them in their private study room. How self-deprecation had twisted her features in an ungainly attempt to mask the hurt he saw in her eyes. Right then, in that moment of hidden vulnerability, Stella Warren had been the most beautiful woman Prince Aleki Esera of Avali had ever seen in his short life.

Sitting across from her now, her professionalism shining as brightly as her sleek ponytail, Aleki wondered further at the kind of man who would choose a dog track over being a part of this incredible woman's life.

"Is this it?"

Stella's voice broke through Aleki's thoughts, as she gestured out the tinted window. Realising the car had come to a stop in the more industrial area of the city, Aleki leaned forward to confirm the building outside was indeed their destination.

In the event supply warehouse, Stella smiled brightly at the young man tending the counter and requested the Warren order. After hoisting two large bags onto the counter, the teen led her out the back like an eager puppy, barely sparing a glance at her royal companion.

Looking as out of place standing in the middle of dusty concrete delivery area as any queen, Stella whipped her smartphone from the pocket of her shorts and fired questions at the older manager who approached them.

Aleki winced in anticipation of the culture clash. Stella's lists and efficiency were in direct contrast to the laid back culture of the island, even in the city.

To his shock, the elderly man answered quickly, in English, and always in the affirmative while Stella ran down a comprehensive list of queries, her red nails flashing in the sun as she scrolled down her phone screen.

"Lotu, you are a magician. Everything is perfect, and you are my hero. I'll see you at ten Wednesday morning for delivery."

"That delivery won't be at my house at ten," Aleki murmured against the soft pink shell of her ear as they moved back through the warehouse, aware of the appreciative gazes of Lotu and his teenage helper glued to Stella's rear.

Satisfaction uncoiled itself like a snake as he noted the shiver that ran through her body. Moving away from him, she hoisted one of the bags from the counter.

"I know. I don't need it until four."

"Island time." Aleki nodded, using the colloquial term to describe the slow moving pace of Avali, along with other tropical Pacific nations. He grabbed the other bag in his hand and heard the soft chink of glass on glass ringing out as the contents moved within it.

"You remembered. Well done, grasshopper."

"The truck will arrive in the afternoon, and I can catalogue and sort. Thursday will be furniture, archway and lighting set up before the pre-wedding picnic and I can do finer details on Friday before the ceremony at five."

With the handle of her own bag tucked into the crook of her elbow, Stella's fingers beat a rhythm against her phone screen as she walked. She smiled up at him, finishing with an emphatic tap on the screen.

"Perfect."

"So what else is on the list for today?"

"Emails, confirmations of travel arrangements, canape and cake selection with the chef at your property, paying the dancers, finalising the cocktail hour playlist, assembling favours and lettering place cards."

"Nothing important then. Excellent." Aleki waited as she nodded to his chauffeur and then slid into the cool interior of the car. "To The Grotto please, Andreas."

"What?" Stella's voice echoed from within the car. "I can't go anywhere else. I have -"

"Cake to taste, emails to send, cars to confirm," Aleki interrupted, his pulse quickening at the glare his guest levelled up towards him from the buttery leather seat of the limo. "And The Grotto to see. It's the new pride of Avali. You would be a remiss tourist indeed to leave without seeing it."

"I'm not here to be a tourist," Stella reminded him, wiggling her way across the seat in a way that caused her breasts to move interestingly beneath her top. "I'm here to create magic. It's bloody hard work creating magic, so forgive me if I don't have time to accompany you on some sightseeing jaunt."

"Some sightseeing jaunt?" Aleki scoffed. "If you're in the business of magic, there's no better place for you to visit."

The limo purred to life underneath them and Andreas pulled smoothly out into the meager mid-morning traffic.

Stella's voice rose higher.

"You don't understand, Aleki. When I say lettering place cards, I mean hand-calligraphing each name onto a banana leaf with gold paint. Do you have any idea how much time that takes?"

"You need to relax, Stella."

The look she gave him would have withered a weaker man. Aleki threw his head back and laughed.

"Look, if you were all alone at a strange venue, I would say fair enough. But the wedding is at my home, Stella. Paolo's coconut cake is exceptional. Choose that. Use the standard canape selection Lani provides for my official engagements. No dance performance group on the island is going to hassle you for payment prior to an event held at my residence. Just take a breath and have some fun for an hour or so, okay?"

Stella inhaled deeply, closed her eyes and looked very much like she was trying not to lose her temper. Then her eyelids snapped open and she fixed him with a malachite stare.

"One hour."

The ride to The Grotto was short, following the main highway that traversed the entire island. After about fifteen minutes, the limo pulled into a deserted rest stop. Indicating she should lead, Aleki noted the tight pull of Stella's shoulders as he followed her down the man-made wooden steps that began by an unobtrusive hand-carved sign that seemed to simply sit by the side of the road.

"If you're going to try to murder me and dump my body, you should know that I started taking Krav Maga a couple of years ago."

Her voice floated back towards him, dragging his attention off the tantalizing sway of her hips.

"Oh, ye of little faith. You'll regret that when you see the treat I have in store for you."

"Oh wow." Stella's reverential tone echoed in the intimacy of the underground cavern when she took the final step. "I'm so sorry I doubted you. I don't even take Krav Maga. Aleki, what *is* this place? It's amazing."

Aleki watched Stella, an anxious twist in the base of his stomach, her eyes roaming over the restaurant set into the natural cave. Tables, covered in crisp white linen meandered along the curve of the cliff edge, while below the ocean lapped at the rugged rock formation. Golden light from the lanterns embedded in the ornate railing spilled onto the polished wooden floorboards, creating a sense of warmth despite the proximity to the water, and emphasising the glint of silverware on the tables.

He had invested in his cousin's restaurant as soon as Sio approached him with the idea. The stunning location, combined with Sio's exquisite food, meant that The Grotto was fast earning a reputation as one of the Pacific's most luxurious dining establishments. Bookings were made months in advance, and the number of proposals the place saw most nights had it rivalling Santorini sunsets for its romance.

Even now, in the still of the day, hours before it opened for evening bookings, the magic of the setting seemed to whisper through the air in time with the light lap of waves at the foundations.

"Aleki!" His cousin's voice rolled through the dining room as he emerged from the discreet door to the kitchen at the far end of the floor.

"It is good to see you, cousin," Aleki responded, stepping into Sio's warm hug. The two embraced firmly.

"*O le fogava'a e tasi.*"

"*O le fogava'a e tasi,*" Sio repeated, patting his cheek.

One family.

Aleki extended a hand towards Stella.

"Sio, I would like you to meet Stella Warren, a friend of mine from New Zealand. Stella, this is my cousin, Sio, owner of The Grotto."

"It's a pleasure to meet you. You have a wonderful place," Stella stepped forward with her hand extended.

Sio brushed it aside and wrapped her in an exuberant embrace.

"Ah, beautiful *palagi*, no handshakes! We are all family here! It is an honour to have you in my restaurant. Please, sit, sit." Sio gestured to the nearest table. "I will be back with treats for you!"

Stella smiled after Sio as he hurried away, her genuine enjoyment of his cousin shining through. Aleki felt a pang resonate as he realised she hadn't looked at him that way since she arrived on the island.

"So, he offered, pouring water from a carafe into the tumblers in front of their place settings, "is this your first time in the Pacific?"

Stella eyed him suspiciously as she lifted her glass to her lips and drank. He tried very hard not to notice the wet sheen of her lips when she returned the glass to the table.

"No," she responded carefully. "I've been to the Cook Islands several times. I've had two weddings there for work and a few holidays."

"With friends?" The desire to know if she'd lain on the beaches with another man suddenly pulled at him.

"Mmm hmmm." A noncommittal answer if ever he heard one. Before he could press the point, she spoke again.

"What is it you do when you're not princing?"

Aleki snorted softly. "There is always princing to be done, fafine aulelei. However, if you're asking about my hobbies, they are few and far between. A little surfing, a little reading, a little fishing."

"Fishing for food, or fishing for women?"

He narrowed his eyes at the crack.

"For food, and for pleasure. Though I will not deny that I have been lucky enough to spend time with some amazing women in the past."

"For more than a night? What witchery those special few must possess."

"There is more than one way to enjoy spending time with the opposite sex. However, my rules are clear. I do not, nor will I, enter into ongoing liaisons."

Stella hitched a single incredulous brow. "So you can date? You can sleep around? You just can't be in a relationship?"

"A relationship is impossible in the life I lead," Aleki insisted.

"Do you ever find it lonely?" Stella's querying tone drew his attention further.

"I am never alone." He hitched a shoulder. "There are always people around me. The opportunities for solitude are slim, and when they occur I treasure them dearly."

Stella lifted her water glass to her lips.

"Don't be obtuse, Aleki. It's beneath you."

Pleasure coursed through him at the challenge and despite himself he felt one corner of his lips tug upward. Stella had always been one to cut through his bravado.

"On occasion," he admitted, his eyes following the long column of her throat as she swallowed. "But the risks outweigh the benefits."

"The risks?" Her eyebrow arched again.

"The potential for scandal. For stories being sold to the press, rumours about the family."

"You really think that would happen?"

"It already has. Avali is a small country. We cannot stand to lose our holdings with other nations. Any whiff of trouble can be enough for them to run scared, to take their deals to the larger islands, Samoa, Tonga, Niue. I will not allow it. The people of Avali work too hard to have their earnings compromised by some scorned lover or column inches in a gossip rag."

Stella sat back in her seat and openly appraised him. A slight curve touched her lips.

"Well, look who's all grown up now."

A chuckle rumbled out of his chest at the not-so-subtle reminder of his wayward party days during his time in Wellington.

"We must all mature sometime. Happily though, for you and I, our looks have remained intact."

His companion snorted.

"Speak for yourself. I prefer to think I've improved with age. God knows, I've spent enough on laser eye surgery to hope so."

"I liked your glasses."

"And I liked you weedy, yet here we sit, with my twenty-twenty vision and your hulking arms."

"Weedy?" Disbelief coloured his tone. "Pacific Islanders are never weedy."

Stella flipped a hand. "Well you certainly didn't resemble a miniature version of The Rock like you do now. With hair, of course," she added generously.

"Of course."

"How lucky for the women of the world that you're unwilling to just settle for exclusivity. One Night With A Prince. It sounds like a film."

"And you? Will they be making a film of your romantic life?"

"They already did. *The Wedding Planner*, with Jennifer Lopez. She runs off with one of the grooms, which is beyond unprofessional. However from memory, the alternative is playing checkers with her dad and she wants more than that. Me, on the other hand? I love checkers."

"But don't you ever find it lonely?" He parroted her earlier question back to her.

A secret smile crept over her face.

"I can date. I can sleep around. I just can't have a relationship."

Jealousy resonated through Aleki's core, a white-hot slash of possessiveness unlike anything he had ever felt before. The idea of another man touching her, of her chesnut hair spread over another man's chest, the rub of her smooth skin over anyone else's body - red flashed behind his eyes and tension ricocheted through his body, coiling his muscles under the fine fabric of his suit.

"And what stops you?" The tightness in his tone betrayed him.

"My career. People think it's all ruffles and canapes, but there's a huge amount of work that goes into each event. In my experience, men don't seem interested in dating a girl who is constantly thinking about weddings, even if it's not her own. I'm never available weekends, won't turn my phone off and refuse their requests to accompany me on work trips like this one." She raised a hand and gestured at their luxurious surroundings. "I *am* Stella Warren Events. It's my name people pay for, my reputation. That's how I support myself. I won't let anything jeopardize that."

"Not even love?"

"Especially not love. Love is beautiful, inspiring, incredible. But it's also unpredictable." Stella's eyes fixed on him and Aleki's heart squeezed at her mask of determination. "I can't risk my livelihood for something so fickle. I cannot change who I am. And finding someone who accepts that is impossible."

"Ah, *fafine aulelei*," Aleki chided. "Life is full of surprises."

"Stop calling me your beautiful woman. I don't do surprises, Aleki. I'm a planner. The word is literally in my job title. The uncertainty, the insecurity of love? That's unacceptable to me."

She paused, tucking a loose strand of hair behind her ear. "I cannot put my happiness in someone else's hands."

Longing flooded Aleki's senses. Longing to reach out, to feel the silk of her dark waves beneath his own fingers. To smooth away the vulnerability that blanketed her with a touch, a kiss. To convince her with his words and his body that she was special - that her fear was unwarranted.

But how could he?

Lust punched through him, tempered by caution. The same caution that had sent him running from New Zealand ten years ago. He wanted Stella, that much was obvious from the electricity that soared through his blood every time their eyes met. But he could not deny his obligations. His responsibility was to the throne and the people of Avali. Whatever craving he felt for the woman in front of him, he could never allow himself to fall for her. One night was all he would ever be able to offer Stella Warren.

THREE

Aleki had attended more than his share of exclusive events, but the lengths Stella had gone to in transforming the wide green lawn at the back of his estate into a luxurious, yet intimate, reception area stole his breath as he surveyed it from his balcony. Silver floor-standing chandeliers marched in uniform succession on either side of one long white-clothed dinner table, throwing golden light over the guests as the muffled sound of laughter soared over the manicured hedges into the warm night. The lights of the nearest village twinkled in the inky beyond, only serving to highlight the joy in his own backyard.

Because of her.

Stella left in two days and as yet, he had not earned her forgiveness or her body. The turning hands of time clawed at his gut. He had been the perfect gentleman all week, even as desire burned in his loins to sweep her up into his arms and feel the hot press of her length against him every time their eyes met over the starched white linens of the breakfast table. He had joined her in the courtyard for breakfast each morning, asking about her job, their mutual friends, her work with a cancer charity. And each morning he dragged himself away with an aching cock and a deepened desire to relive their single night of pleasure. She avoided him the rest of the time - their work kept them apart during the day but in the evenings when he went looking for her Lani had informed him she had retired early to her room with a plate of grilled fish and vegetables.

A smile tugged at his lips. *Smart thinking, little star.* The electricity between them could generate enough power for the sound system she'd hired for tonight's traditional island dance performance. But while he chased it, craved it, Stella was hiding from it. Aleki knew better than anyone that fear of facing a situation only escalated the stakes of the outcome.

Descending to the lawn, he snagged two glasses from the glittering champagne tower that rose like Aphrodite out of a sea of frangipani. Holding the coupes carefully, he made his way to the side of the blond wood dance floor constructed in the middle of the white hibiscus garden. A cool rush of air settled his nerves as he breathed in deeply, the familiar scent of the ocean calming the pulse which pounded at his wrist in time with the song pounding out of the nearby speakers.

Stella seemed unaware of his approach as she stood swaying gently under the pergola hidden to the side. He took a moment to study the way the moonlight cut shadows across her fine cheekbones, making her eyes appear luminous and catching the muted sparkle of her black sequin cocktail dress. The one-shouldered design was demure, emphasising the graceful length of her arms, while the hem hit below the knee, showcasing her toned calves. Yet, despite the dress's attempts to cover her body, Aleki's palms tingled at the thought of the lush curves hidden beneath the delicate fabric.

Swallowing around the nervous lump in his throat, he took three steps out of the shadows until he stood before Stella.

"To you." He extended one of the glasses.

Her full lips, painted a rich ruby, lifted as she accepted the proffered champagne coupe.

"To me." The clink of their toast echoed gently in Aleki's ears as he raised the glass to his lips and gulped down a healthy swallow of the refreshingly dry vintage.

Stella followed suit, and Aleki's blood stirred as an errant drop of champagne clung to her crimson bottom lip.

Unaware, she turned the full force of her wide eyes on him.

"What do you think of the wedding?"

"It's beautiful, Stella." His voice throbbed low with intensity, and he caught the glow of pride in her eyes as she smiled in response.

"I've never seen Mae and Luke so happy." He gestured with his glass to where the newlyweds were shimmying to an upbeat number on the dance floor.

Stella beamed, and he couldn't resist any longer.

"Dance with me."

Her eyes widened and darted immediately to the left.

"I have to - the caterer -"

"Stella." He waited until she looked at him directly again, her perfect white teeth worrying the soft pad of her lower lip.

"Dance with me."

Hesitating slightly, she took the hand he offered and stepped out of the gazebo into the light of the dancefloor. As he escorted her onto the floor, the music changed and the first gentle strums of Tiki Taane's 'Always On My Mind' floated across the garden.

Aleki felt one side of his mouth lift as the irony of dancing with Stella to a song he always associated with his time in New Zealand settled over him, as palpable as the acoustic reggae beat of the song itself.

Finding an unoccupied spot near the edge of the dance-floor, Aleki pulled her into his arms.

Finally.

The tension that had thrummed between his shoulder blades since opening his door to her on Sunday evening eased as his breath whooshed out in a glorious exhalation.

Nothing could compare to this. There was no match for the feel of Stella's warm body pressed against him, for the smooth weight of her hand in his, the cool brush of her breath over his knuckles as he sandwiched their joined hands against his chest.

An intensely male pull of satisfaction at having the woman he wanted in his arms after almost a week of waiting tugged at his heart.

"Stella?" Gently, with infinite tenderness, he stroked the pad of this thumb across the back of her hand.

"Mmmm?"

"Can you feel that?" He pressed her palm against the hard expanse of his chest, above the rapid cadence of his heart.

Her fingertips fluttered over his flesh, rending a groan from his throat as her cautious exploration sparked a flurry of sensations sparking through him, alighting his senses.

"Yes."

Was it his imagination, or was her voice breathier than normal?

"That's what you do to me." Leaning down, he placed his lips against the soft shell of her ear and whispered.

"You make me burn."

Slowly she raised her gaze to meet him, the deep pools of her irises reflecting his own desire back to him.

"Aleki..." Her voice trailed off, and he took her silence as the opportunity it was.

"I never stopped wanting you, Stella. Even after all these years, nobody has ever affected me this way."

He moved closer, pulling her against his chest and letting her feel the evidence of his yearning between them. The crisp scent of her perfume teased at his nostrils, mixing with the tang of the lagoon beyond the party.

"Wanting isn't the issue, Aleki."

"Then what is, *fafine aulelei*? Neither of us are seeking love, but here, in this moment, is passion not enough?"

Scarlet lips parted on an intake of breath, and he seized his chance. Tracing a finger softly along the elegant arch of her brow he felt her tremble. The rich playground of her mouth was within inches. Leaning down, he brushed his lips over hers, a fleeting touch that scorched through his entire being like an electric charge.

Lifting his head, despite the magnetic pull low in his gut to claim her mouth, her body, as his own, he exhaled deeply.

"There is nobody I have felt such passion for in all my years, *fafine aulelei*."

Indecision warred in Stella's gaze, and the desire he saw in its depth bolstered his confidence.

"Just once, Stella? Let me taste the stars."

Aleki returned his mouth to hers and smiled against the rich nirvana of her lips as he felt her hesitation ebb. The tension drained from her body with every nip, every nibble as he feasted upon her. Adrenaline surged in his veins as

Stella's fingers tightened around the cage of his arms and she kissed him back with fervor. He plunged into the sweet heaven of her mouth, stroking her tongue with his in a rhythm born of desire. His hands bunched against the fabric cloaking her hips, grinding his pelvis against hers as though he could brand her with his need through the barrier of their clothes. She moaned softly and bucked against him, the press of her stomach firm against the raging column of his erection. *Gods, yes.* She rolled her hips again, rubbing and grinding, sending stars spinning behind his eyelids as the sensation raced over his cock and up his body, hot and tight and dizzying in its intensity. He wrenched his lips from her, harsh pants painting the air around them. A quick glance around confirmed that the song had ended, blending into an old school country number that had distracted all the other dancefloor inhabitants into an intensive sing-a-long in the middle of the floor. Nobody was watching them.

Aleki looked down at Stella, his eyes searching her face for any evidence of discomfort. He found none. The heat in her gaze was enough to melt glaciers. He flushed as it hit him square in the chest, radiating warmth down to the place where their bodies still pressed together. He ground slowly, just a little press of his hips against hers and saw affirmation in the hitch of her chest, the bite of her lip.

Mine again, after all this time.

"Come, little star," he whispered in her ear. "We have some unfinished business to attend to."

THE WALK ACROSS THE LAWN, through the foyer and up the stairs gave Stella plenty of time to resume her sanity but not once did she come close to saying no. The light touch of Aleki's hand on her back as he escorted her acted as a touchstone, keeping her grounded on the mission even as her hormones whizzed around her in overt glee and her brain warned against following them into the blissful abyss.

He'll never love you. He's told you as much.

Shut up, Stella scolded her dour brain. *We've had plenty of sex without love before. Let me have this. Just once more.*

"Holy shit." The gasp tumbled from Stella's lips on impact as her back hit her bedroom door with a thud. Aleki's body covered hers, hard and unyielding, his breath hot on her throat.

"Still with me, little star?" He sucked a scorching open mouthed kiss onto the delicate skin of her neck, his fingers tunneling under her dress and grazing up her thighs to grasp at her arse.

"Still with you," she managed, bucking her hips forward into the glorious bulge in his pants.

His groan echoed through the high ceilinged hallway. "*Stella.*" Her name rang out like a benediction as he kneaded her flesh, his strong hands anchoring her to him as he rubbed himself against the silk of her underwear.

"Stop teasing me, Aleki. I need you." She'd have been embarrassed by the admission if she were capable of feeling anything beyond blind lust.

Aleki dropped his face to the curve of her shoulder once more, the scrape of teeth over her collarbone sending sparks of urgency shooting through her, her nipples like diamonds against the smooth lining of her dress.

"You need me, little star?" His question rasped over the hollow of her throat. "Do you need to remember how it feels to have me inside you? To be filled so completely you can't think, can't speak, can't do anything but take the pleasure I give you?"

"Please, Aleki. *Please.*"

He moved one hand from her body and to open the door Aleki's lips parted from her bare shoulder and hungry, obsidian eyes

"The bed."

She moved quickly, desperation hurrying her steps.

"Stop."

"But-"

"Stay there."

Stella shifted her weight from foot to foot, one hand already on the headboard. Blood roared through her as the ache to be filled pulsed beneath the thin silk of her underwear.

Hot awareness throbbed low in her as Aleki swept the soft fall of her hair over towards her exposed shoulder. His lips brushed the opposite side of her neck, sending goose-bumps skittering across her chest. He kissed and nuzzled the tender flesh, teasing her with a swipe of his tongue, the scrape of his teeth. The hand holding her hair fell to the discreet tab of the zipper under her arms, and he lowered it slowly, the sound of each dainty tooth sawing open filling the air like the rumble of a Formula One race. The dress dropped slowly, a tangle of sequins at her heels.

Strong brown arms pulled her back against the naked planes of his torso. His navy suit was gone, she realised, along with the white shirt she'd grasped during their dance floor kiss. His body was hot and strong at her back, the crisp hair on his chest and the powerful thighs bracketing her legs tickling deliciously against her skin. She rubbed backwards gently, and was rewarded with a growl.

"You make me forget myself."

"Good." Stella panted. "Forgetting you is one of my hobbies."

He laughed, low and wicked in her ear as his hands stroked slowly up her ribs to fan along the underside of her breasts.

"You never really forget though do you, little star?" Talented fingers tugged at a nipple and she moaned. "That's why you're here now. Because you know what I can do to your body. If someone else could do it, you'd be with him. But here you are, back with me, wanting what only I can give you."

"Hurry up and give it to me, then." Stella's voice was as husky as his as she arched her back, thrusting out her chest and grinding back against him. "Because for someone who promised me action, you're doing an awful lot of talking."

"That mouth is going to get you into trouble one day." The callused fingertips of one hand trailed down her stomach, the slight abrasions firing through her even as his touch gentled below her stomach, travelling in teasing circles over her hips and the top of her thighs.

Jesus, she could barely breathe, the anticipation had her strung so tight. He slipped his hand under the thin barrier of her underwear, one long finger swiping through her folds up to the sensitive bundle of nerves and circled it slowly. She whimpered - *whimpered* - and jerked her hips forward, seeking more.

A ragged breath razed her ear. "Oh, my star. Do you think you can control this? That's very sweet."

Fuck this. She spun in his arms, twisting their bodies so the prince was situated next to the bed. One firm shove and he fell to a sitting position on the mattress.

"Is that what you think, Aleki? That this will be like the last time?" Stella mocked, throwing one leg over his heavy thighs and straddling his lap. Hunger licked at her from the shadows of his eyes, the challenge apparent. She ran her fingers across the breadth of his shoulders, the tight muscles bunching under her touch. "The worldly prince and the sweet little virgin?" Her laugh dripped like poison as she rocked her hips against the erection straining the front of his boxer briefs. "Have you learned nothing about me this week?" Bending her head, she tugged Aleki's earlobe between her teeth, lightly pulling the tender flesh in time with the rhythm of her thrusts. A tortured moan filled the air as his hands came up to grasp at her cheeks, settling her more fully onto his lap.

"I control *everything*. You want inside me?" She swiped her tongue up his neck, exalting in the tang of sweat that coated her taste buds. "Then listen to me when I say *stop fucking around and get there*."

She was on her back in an instant, the comforter cool at her back as frenzied hands ripped her underwear down her legs and over the black heels she still wore. Aleki shoved his own underwear down, fisting himself roughly before he fell on her, licking, sucking, biting her breasts, thrusting his erection into the vee of her thighs and rubbing the crown through her slick folds. Holding his dark head to her chest, she bucked her hips against his as the tip of his cock rubbed against her sweet spot.

"Like that, *fafine aulelei*? Like that?"

"God, yes. Condom. Hurry." Her words came fast, desperate as he pushed her closer to the edge.

He was gone for a second and she could hear him rifling through his pockets as one hand drifted down between her legs to settle against the hard knot of her desire, before her hand was knocked away.

"I would give half the kingdom to watch you take your

own pleasure, little star. But right now I'm too close. When I come tonight, it will be inside you." The sound of ripping foil followed in the wake of Aleki's growled - *promise? Threat?* - and then he was there, the luscious weight of him pressing her to the mattress as he notched himself at her entrance and sealed his mouth to hers.

Then slowly, slowly, slowly, he eased into her, each inch of him dragging through her, thick and purposeful. A delicious torture, sliding deep and deliberately until he was seated fully inside her. Easing up onto his hands, he held his weight above her and trapped her with his eyes.

"Is that what you wanted, little star?"

Aleki. Staring at me, hair flopping over his forehead, muscles tensed. Inside me, filling me.

"Yes." Her words were tight, high, born from the tension coiled down where their bodies joined and leaking out through her lips, unfiltered and real. "Yes, that's what I want."

"Good. Then that's what you'll get." Aleki began to move, sliding almost out of her and then burying himself to the hilt, grinding his pelvis against hers when he seated, brushing his crisp curls against her nub.

Bliss rolled over her, a thick golden blanket, as he pumped inside her. She raised her hips, matching him thrust for thrust, triumphing in the knowledge that the bite of her heels were digging into his arse even as he lowered his head to deliver a deep, pulling suck to her nipple. The haze doubled, the line between pleasure and power as they fought together, pushed and pulled together, chasing euphoria. One of Aleki's hands dropped, grasping her butt cheek with bruising fingers as he knocked her knee upwards with his own, opening her up and tilting his hips and gliding up to hit her perfectly. The change of angle blinded Stella, and she squeezed her eyes shut, every thought in her head falling out of her mouth in one long continuous gasp as she rocketed towards the edge of the cliff. "*Oh my God, like that, please Aleki, don't stop, I need it, I need you, just like that, right there, right there, please.*"

With a final swirl of his tongue around the tender flesh of her nipple, she felt Aleki's head raise up from her chest.

"Stella." Her name on his lips was harsh, guttural. "Open your eyes, little star. Look at me."

Wrenching her lids open, Stella met his gaze, hot and desperate. Fire flashed in the depths of his eyes as he stared down at her, his breath ragged as he bore down, twisting his hips as he drove home. Caught in the web of his stare, Stella could do nothing to stem the tidal wave of pleasure that rose up inside her, ruthless and twisting, coiling tight behind her abdomen. Aleki tightened his grip and surged forward and the dam broke, a thousand sparkling pieces shattering behind her eyes as she flew, pleasure shooting like stars under her skin. She cried out and from somewhere beyond the rainbow in her head heard her name being chanted in rough pants as Aleki followed her into the void.

FOUR

"I'm dying."

Stella flopped face down on the turquoise leather couch in Mae's open plan living area and groaned heartily.

"What is it this time?" Behind the breakfast bar Mae flicked the jug on and pulled two brightly patterned mugs out of a cupboard. "Tulips in autumn? A five course gourmet meal for under a thousand bucks?"

"The mother-in-laws," Stella grumbled, burrowing her face into a cheery yellow throw pillow. "Always the bloody mother-in-laws. I don't have the strength for it today."

"You have the strength for anything," Mae claimed airily, pulling the milk out of the fridge.

"Not today. I'm exhausted. I threw up twice before the dress shopping and then had to spend ninety minutes listening to Mrs Rawiri bemoan the lack of modesty in young women today while she vetoed every decent dress in her daughter-in-law's budget." Stella rolled over onto her back, so she could see Mae pouring the water for the tea.

Sweet, sweet tea.

"I can't believe how tan you still are," she continued as

Mae set the kettle back on the counter. "It's been nearly two months since the wedding and you look like you just got back from Avali."

Mae ignored her. "You threw up?"

"Twice. It was revolting."

"Are you pregnant?"

"Of course not," Stella scoffed, even as apprehension slid along her spine.

Mae levelled her with a look.

"No?"

"No." Stella replied firmly.

"Prove it." Mae rummaged through her handbag on the kitchen counter.

Instinctively, Stella caught the item that was tossed her way.

"A pregnancy test? Why do you have this in your handbag?"

Mae shrugged.

"I'm a newlywed. Those things are like breath mints to us. You gotta keep them everywhere just in case."

Sighing, Stella rose from the couch and headed towards the bathroom.

Eight weeks since the wedding. Did I have a period in there? Surely. But they're irregular anyway. Jessie's little brother was in the office last week when he was too sick to go to school. Could I have caught something off him?

Ablutions completed, she returned to the couch.

"What if it's positive?" Mae's voice was kind as she handed Stella her tea.

"It won't be. I'm just taking this to get you off my case."

Two minutes later, Stella stared in disbelief at two very pink lines in the test window. Panic swelled in her, tightening her chest and churning a tight, hot roil in her stomach.

Oh my god, oh my god, oh my god.

Mae patted her shoulder.

"Congratulations, mama."

Stella swallowed thickly.

"You're not seeing anyone?"

"No," Stella replied faintly. Her voice sounded very far away.

"Okay." Mae hopped off the couch and rummaged in her bag again, coming up with her phone.

In the background, Stella could hear Mae making an appointment with her doctor as the fuzz in her head slowly cleared.

Right, the doctor. That made sense. What else?

To do list. Doctor. Confirmation. Freak the eff out.

Mae thumbed off her phone and tossed it on the counter as she made her way back to the couch. "Wednesday at ten. The benefits of having the same doctor huh?"

"Lucky me." Her voice was as hollow as her stomach.

"Lucky you. So. You know I have to ask..." Mae hesitated and Stella arched an eyebrow at her. "The father?"

Nausea rose in Stella's throat again, the metallic note clanging against her tastebuds, filling her mouth with the tang of regret and fear.

"Just a guy."

Mae's eyebrows shot skywards.

"Just a guy?" Incredulity laced her voice. "Not Steve-The-Plumber or Mountain-Goat-Carson who wouldn't trim his fingernails or Chris-On-The-Beach-At-New-Years? You always have a name."

Stella shrugged, guilt washing over her.

"Just a guy."

"Right," Mae drew the word out sarcastically. "Just a guy. Like the guy you lost your virginity to. He was just a guy too, right?

Stella winced, and Mae's eyes widened.

"Oh my god. They're the *same* guy. It's Aleki, isn't it?"

Silence hung in the air as Stella examined the contents of her mug of tea with abnormal interest.

"I should have known." A thread of accusation ran through Mae's voice. "You left Avali the day after the wedding, and you've never once left a holiday early before. Not even when you got food poisoning in Brunei and lost six kilos in a week."

"I was sick," Stella insisted, gripping her mug as the lie rolled off her tongue.

"Sick of being stuck in the same house as your ex, maybe," Mae retorted. "How could you not tell me this at uni? Oh my god, Stel, I asked you to stay at his *house* for a week to organise the wedding. I would never have done that if I'd known!"

Resigned to her fate, Stella shrugged and sipped her tea.

"It is what it is. Your wedding was more important than my feelings."

"Well obviously not all of your feelings," Mae observed drily. "Because there must have been a bit of *feeling* going on to wind up in this predicament."

"You're not funny."

"I'm hilarious. But seriously, Stel-" Mae's voice sombered. "What are you going to do?"

Stella sank her head into her hands, as images of potential outcomes assuaged her like fuzzy Polaroids. A sterile hospital environment. Going home to an empty apartment. Continuing her life as she knew it but never knowing what could have been. Opening her door in twenty years to a grown man or woman whose name she didn't even know, seeking a connection, an explanation from her. A brown-skinned baby kicking its legs on the middle of a sheepskin rug in the middle of her living room.

How much do sheepskin rugs cost?

"I have no idea," she admitted, the words whooshing out of her like air from a balloon, leaving a sense of deflation behind. "This wasn't part of the plan."

STICK TO THE PLAN.

Aleki strode out of the elevator onto the open walkway of the apartment complex, inhaling the crisp winter air deeply. Neither the flight from Avali, the car from the airport or the urine-scented contraption that had delivered him to the building's fourth floor had allowed him to take in enough air to centre himself. Not that finding a calm moment had been easy since he'd received the phone call late last night. Anger pulsed through him at the memory.

"*Malo?*"

"You stupid bastard."

"Luke?"

"You selfish prick."

"Are you upset?" The question was mild, because similar accusations had been made before, in reference to anything from purchasing an antique Turkish rug for the spare bedroom to taking the last beer from the cooler.

"How could you shag Mae's *best friend*-" Luke's voice pitched with anger "and not use a condom?"

"I did use a condom." The surprise that had bloomed in

his chest at Luke's knowledge of his night with Stella tightened into a hard ball of unease.

Wait. What?

"Why would you think I didn't use a condom, Luke?"

Silence.

"*Luke?*"

A heavy sigh.

"She's pregnant."

"*Leai.*"

The denial slipped past his frozen lips before he could stop it. Cold flooded his body, the icy tendrils roping over his chest and down his forearms, tunneling ahead of the fear that rushed in its wake.

"No." He forced the English translation out through the tightness in his throat. "It's not possible." He was careful, always.

"Well, according to Mae, there's a trio of pregnancy tests from this afternoon proving you wrong, my man. Look, I don't know if I was supposed to say anything, but my wife is storming around the house threatening to unman you."

The fear bubbled, shifted, a moving entity that danced in the face of his dismay. Luke kept speaking, but Aleki heard nothing but the rush of blood in his ears as the implications settled themselves into his consciousness.

Stella, pregnant. A baby. His baby. His heir.

Oh God, his father.

"I have to go." He cut Luke off mid-sentence. "Thank you for calling. I'll be in touch." He hung up without waiting for a reply as his brain whirred through the likely responses of King Tama of Avali reacting to news of his first grandchild. None of them were good.

It had taken a sleepless night to organise an unscheduled trip to Wellington without his father finding out, but it was done. He was here, he had a plan, and the sooner he stopped loitering in the outdoor hallway like a well-dressed Jehovah's Witness and got on with it the better.

He strode down the walkway, the tap of his shoes echoing off the terracotta coloured tiles. For the eighth time since landing, he checked the address Luke had texted through. Apartment 12. He came across it at the end of the hall, and rapped briskly on the door under the brass numbers. A faint groan sounded through the door several beats before it cracked open.

"Aleki?" Shock coloured Stella's tone as she swung the door wider, revealing herself in full.

Her chestnut waves were up in a short fountain on the top of her head and she wore nothing he could see other than a black oversize sweatshirt than hit the top of her thighs and a pair of white sports socks. Desire punched low in his gut, heating his skin. His cock twitched in his pants and if he felt electrified by her presence, she looked as though she'd been struck by lightning at his. Wide green eyes did little to distract from the pallour under her light tan, but the end result was certainly that of a woman who was unhappy to see him.

Well, too bad.

Aleki strode past her into the apartment, turning his hips a little to accommodate the fact that she remained in the doorway like she was glued to the spot. Sweeping his eyes over the apartment, he catalogued the clean lines of the modern furniture and monochrome decor. Only a single vase of lavender roses on the coffee table stopped him from thinking he'd been transported back to the black-and-white world of Dorothy's Kansas. Glancing towards the kitchen, he could see a similar situation - devoid of both colour and clutter, save for a small plate with the remnants of cheese and crackers by the sink.

"No, please, come in." Stella's sarcasm washed over Aleki like a wave as she shut the door and turned to face him. She raised an eyebrow at him haughtily and Aleki was struck again by how in control she seemed, even now with a royal ex-lover barging into her home while she was half-clothed. He let his eyes linger over the toned length of her legs, reaching up, up, up until they reached the thick cotton of her sweatshirt, brushing the top of her thighs just higher than was decent. If she raised her arms, he'd be able to see her panties...

"Your Highness." Stella's tone could have cut diamonds. "I doubt you flew halfway across the Pacific to stare at my legs. What do you want?"

The tension that had been simmering in Aleki's shoulders since Luke's call unfurled throughout his torso, creeping lower and lower until his chest tightened with suppressed emotion.

"Your legs, little star, are worth crossing more than a single ocean." He stalked towards her. "Or perhaps you think I have forgotten how they felt locked around me? *Leai, fafine aulelei.* No man forgets the feel of heaven."

He heard the hitch of her breath, music to his ears as she pressed her back against the closed door. He moved closer, electricity sparkling like champagne in the space between their bodies. The cool citrus scent of her perfume teased his nostrils, and he drew a deep breath, taking in as much of her scent as he could. Memories flashed, the last time he'd seen her awake, smelt her, wearing this perfume, black heels and nothing else. Rocking into him, lush and ripe and dizzyingly perfect.

"Why are you here, Aleki?" Stella's voice was little more than a whisper.

"You know why I am here, little star. You left my home before we could talk. And now it appears you have taken something of mine with you."

Stella's eyes fell shut and he felt the loss of their green light like a fist to his gut. She muttered something under her breath that sounded suspiciously like "Fucking Luke."

"You are pregnant?"

"I think so." She held up a hand at his grumble of discontent. "I've taken some tests that have come up positive, but I need a blood test to be confident. I'm seeing the doctor the day after tomorrow and I'll know for sure then."

"And what do you plan to do if you are?"

Stella let out a groan. "Let's sit down."

He let her lead him back to the living area and sank onto the squashy white linen couch that reminded him disconcertingly of a giant marshmallow. Stella bundled herself up in a black blanket at the opposite end, hiding her legs from view. He mourned the loss.

"Honestly, Aleki, I don't know what to do. My business is going so well right now, but it isn't the kind of career that works well with a baby. I can't commit to a boyfriend, remember? Let alone a child for the rest of my life. I'd need a two-bedroom apartment, and I can't afford that-"

"Money would be no object."

Stella shot him a wan smile. "That's kind of you to say Aleki, but the reality is that I can't do this on my own. If I decide not to terminate, there's always adoption. Brad and Oscar Reynolds did that after they got married and they have the cutest little boy now."

"You would give our baby away?" A protective pull tugged at the centre of his chest as he glanced towards the mass of black fabric swaddling her stomach and hiding it from his view.

"Possibly." She sighed again, an anxious look creasing her brow. "I know how it feels to be unwanted by a parent, but this way I could give our child a family that really did truly want it. That happens a lot in the islands too, doesn't it?"

"To *family*." Aleki couldn't keep the horror from his voice. The Polynesian practice of *whangai* meant children were often raised by extended family members if their own parents felt unable to care for them. "Not to *strangers*."

"Well I don't have any family here, Aleki," Stella snapped. "Unless you want your son or daughter to be raised by my deadbeat father and half the local pub."

Now. Do it now.

Aleki sucked in a deep breath. "There is one other option, Stella."

She shot him a sulky glare. "What?"

"Marry me."

FIVE

Stella flipped her laptop screen down and rubbed her temples. Most of the four hour flight from Wellington to Avali on Aleki's family jet had been spent rescheduling meetings, updating her documents and organising professional development for Jessie, her assistant who would be stepping into her shoes while Stella was in the islands.

A fortnight wasn't a huge amount of time in most careers, but weddings moved fast even in the off-season. *Thank God I didn't get knocked up in January.* Mae and Luke had taken advantage of the all-round sunshine of Avali to hold their wedding in the middle of New Zealand's miserable winter, which meant her planning work was intense but the actual number of events low. Aleki had badgered her into carving out two weeks on the island to plead his case for their proposed marriage.

Not that she needed too much convincing. As an only child with abandonment issues, her psychosis had been halfway to agreeing on the spot. The concept of two parents, a loving family, time and resources to devote to their son or daughter's upbringing? Yes, yes and yes! She was fortunate the rational part of her brain had stepped in to stop the scared little girl inside of her being in charge of any big kid decisions. Literally.

"Would you like some water?"

Stella glanced across the aisle at Aleki.

"No, thank you. How much longer do you think we'll be in the air?"

"Only another thirty minutes or so, I would venture. Are you sure about the water? Your blood volume has increased by fifty percent since you conceived. Dehydration is a concern."

What the ever-loving heck?

"My blood?"

"Yes. Your body produces more blood when you are pregnant. It's extraordinary. Would you like to read about it?"

Tapping his phone screen, he held it out to her so that she could see the loading screen for a popular pregnancy app.

"I'm okay, thanks."

To Do List. Download pregnancy app. Drink more water, apparently. Get better at knowing your own body than your baby daddy.

"If you say so."

"What should I expect in Avali?" The concern that had been haunting her since her agreement to fly back with Aleki burst forth from her mouth in a rush.

Aleki's mouth tightened in a grim line. "It will be different. Our people, our welcoming culture will remain the same. But coming home with me? That will stir some talk." Deep brown eyes caught hers and pinned her in place with the warring emotions she saw there. "I have never brought a woman back to Avali with me."

"Do you keep a stable full of them there?" Stella's attempt at light delivery stumbled and tripped over her own tongue, landing clumsily in the space between them.

"*Leai*, little star. You are determined to think the worst of me. Avali is my home. It is where I take refuge. My role as prince is one that I take seriously, because failure to do so is to fail my people. Whatever, *whomever*, I may entertain myself with on foreign soil, when I am in Avali I am here to serve. I have never been romantically linked to a woman on the island, and I have never brought a woman with whom I am romantically linked onto the island."

He could hear her gulp, she was sure of it.

"So this is a first for both of us?"

"It is different, and what is different is always exciting to begin with." Aleki shrugged a single shoulder and Stella tried not to salivate at the simple bunch and pull of the lean muscles under his dress shirt. "There will be some interest, more so when we announce our engagement."

"The engagement I have yet to agree to?"

"It will happen. You remember our discussion about the tabloids. I cannot bring shame upon my family. The social and economic fallout would be too great. If you remain pregnant, you will do so as my wife."

Fury rose in her throat like a wave.

"Shame?" The word came out low, dangerous. *We'll get to my bodily rights later.*

Aleki sighed, the timbre of his voice aligning with the dip of the plane as they began their descent.

"Shame is a different beast in the islands, *fafine aulelei*. In the *palagi* world, shame is fleeting, a bad idea that sits with one for awhile and slowly fades. Shame in Polynesia is a living thing. It encompasses families, wrapping tighter around them until it is like a curse. Everyone knows and nothing absolves it. Not time, not deed, not a new generation. The people of Avali are progressive in many ways, little star, but this is not one of them. We are a culture where family comes first. Allowing my child to be born out of wedlock would bring that shame on my family, on our *pepe*. It would be unacceptable regardless of my status, but as it is, the royal family would lose face not only with our people, but across the Pacific. I cannot permit that."

"And if I abort? Avali doesn't seem like the kind of country that is super progressive in terms of reproductive rights."

"We are a religious country, yes. While we fought off the colonisers who tried to claim our land for their own, the values of Christianity aligned with our own in a way that the ancestors embraced. However, it is your choice whether you keep this baby or not. You are the one who will need to grow this child, to care for it until others can do so. I would not presume to tell you what to do with your body."

Relief rushed through Stella, leaving her almost dizzy in its wake. She'd been avoiding the question, aware of the strong religious culture in the Pacific, but hearing Aleki's assertion that she should make her choice as she saw fit assuaged anxieties she hadn't been aware she was holding until this minute.

The jolt of wheels on tarmac roused her out of her thoughts, and she busied herself packing away her laptop and headphones while Aleki remained still in the plush, toffee coloured seats, staring out the window as the plane taxied along the runway of the Havalei'i airport. Aleki had explained on the flight that the royal family owned a private aircraft, but private airstrips were considered an extravagance when the land could be used to grow crops or house livestock that would boost the island's economy.

The plane coasted to a stop and Stella adjusted her dress, smoothing her hands over the white linen as nerves jangled in her throat.

"*Fafine aulelei?*"

She looked up to see Aleki standing above her, his white shirt and charcoal dress pants crisp and his hand extended. For a moment she just stared, taking in the dark pool of his eyes, the sharp line of his jaw, the burnished tone of his skin. The two days since Aleki had arrived in her doorway had been such a blur that she hadn't had a moment to look, really look, at the father of her baby. Awareness flared to life inside her as she took him in, from the warmth of his gaze, to the pads of his exceptionally capable hands. The combination of the boy she'd once harboured a crush on and the man she lusted after now. Slipping her hand into his, she let him guide her out of her seat towards the door.

"There is a small welcome prepared, as is customary for all arrivals. You will have experienced something similar at the airport last time you visited, but due to my position this will be a little more formal."

"I thought the point of a private plane was to avoid attention."

Aleki grinned, and heat flared in Stella's core.

Down, girl.

"Avoiding attention has never been my strong suit, little star. But no, this reception is nothing more than business as usual. Hospitality is the bedrock of the Pacific. Every airport in Polynesia will welcome travellers in some way. It is what we know. It is who we are."

With that, the doors opened. The warmth of the air whooshed into the cabin, conjuring images of beaches and cocktails even within the small space. Aleki stepped into the light, tugging her forward with him as they descended the plane.

The beat of traditional island drums soared through the air, reverberating through her and stirring her senses as her heart raced to keep up with the strike of wood on wood. In front of the plane on the tarmac, oiled dancers dressed in *tapa* cloths wrapped around them from the waist down swirled and stomped in time with the music. The beaten barkcloths were etched with traditional designs in brown, black and red, complimenting the colouring of the dancers and the barbed crimson necklaces they wore. Behind the men, a line of female dancers swayed and undulated, wrapped in a rainbow of silks and leis. Their gentle movements worked in tandem with the intensity of the men, and their clear, high voices reached Stella even over the fierce beat of the drum. The performance engulfed Stella, overwhelming her senses as the air pulsed with the beat of the drums, the scent of the ocean beyond the runway and her body thrummed in awareness of Aleki's hand in hers. His eyes were fixed on the dancers below, eyes shimmering and his free hand clasped on his chest as his people welcomed him home.

He'd show that kind of love for our child. She had seen it in his eyes when he spoke of their baby, the same ferocity that shone now as he surveyed his subjects with pride and passion pulsing through him.

The music stopped abruptly, the men on one knee, heads bowed, facing the plane, and in the silence she heard Aleki's words in her head.

We are a country where family comes first.

"Fine," she whispered, leaning into him as the echo of the drums faded into the air above them. "I'll marry you."

UNTIL THAT MOMENT, Aleki Esera would swear he
had never felt joy. There had been good times, certainly.
The thrill of skydiving, the satisfaction of negotiating trade
deals, the delight of a woman in his bed. But not until he
stood on Avali soil, watching his people greet him and
clasping the hand of the woman who would bear both his
child and his name had he experienced such a surfeit of
pure joy. Elated, he turned to the woman by his side.

"You will not regret this," he swore, clutching their
clasped hands to his chest. His heartbeat swelled beneath
his breastbone, pounding against his ribcage as he stared
deep into her eyes, trying to imprint his solemnity on her
soul.

Stella offered him a shy smile, and his shoulders softened
as warmth crept over him that had nothing to do with the
tropical island temperature. She was stubborn and independent, his Stella, and she had chosen *him*, Aleki Esera, to be
her husband when she did not need or particularly want one.

I will not let her down.

"Your Highness?"

"Lani!" His emotions made him more effusive than
usual, and his assistant frowned at his uncharacteristic
animation.

"It's lovely to see you again, Lani." Stella stepped
forward smoothly, greeting the other woman with a kiss on
the cheek. "I adore your outfit. That colour is fantastic on
you."

They stood together, the two most important women in
his life, one in swirls of orange and one in a modest white
shirtdress that looked no worse the wear for a four-hour

flight. The sheer rightness of having two such formidable allies standing beside him settled in his gut.

You can do this. You can be the leader your people need. All you have to do is show him.

As if reading his thoughts, Lani turned to him.

"His Majesty has requested your presence. *Loto'a.*"

Even without Lani's raised eyebrow, the significance was not lost on him.

"I see."

"What do you see?" Stella looked between them, her green eyes wide.

"*Loto'a* means 'inside the fence'," Aleki explained. "It is the local reference for the palace. Out of respect for the royal family, the people of Avali rarely say the word 'palace' itself. King Tama has several residences on the island, but he is summoning us to the seat of his power. It means he is not happy with me."

"What could you have possibly done wrong?" Stella raised her eyebrows comically and her grin sent a shower of sparks through him. He reached his hand out and seized her wrist, pulling her warm body against his and dropping a light kiss on her lips. Ignoring the gasps from the dancers who were milling around, he smiled down at his woman.

"Nothing, little star. I have done absolutely nothing wrong."

"Be that as it may, the king is waiting." Aleki tore his eyes off Stella and turned reluctantly to Lani, whose side-eye could win championships.

"Indeed." He brushed invisible lint off his grey dress shirt. "Let us not waste any more of His Majesty's time."

The car purred along the highway as Aleki turned the new developments over in his head. In the background he could hear Stella chatting with Lani and asking Andreas about his family, sparkling with the spirit that had first attracted him to her - that had *always* attracted him to her. And that was what was causing the queasiness in his stomach, the throb of blood at his temples. Now that he had Stella, he could see - it was always her he had been waiting for. He had run from it at university, but here they were years later, in the very place he had known they would end up if he stayed.

"We're here."

Lani's pronouncement cut through his turmoil.

"Oh," Stella breathed beside him, clutching at his arm. "It's beautiful."

Her eyes were wide as the car passed through the ornate gates and she gazed out at the manicured lawns leading down to the sea.

"The building was erected in 1857," Lani intoned. "It is crafted from the wood of local trees. Bedrooms are on the second floor, with the receiving rooms and diplomatic chambers below. Our National Archives are housed in the east wing and are open to the public during the week. The white walls and red roof reflect the colours of the Avali flag."

"It looks almost European," Stella observed, leaning forward to peer out the window. Several strands of hair fell across her face and Aleki reached out to tuck them back behind her ear, relishing the cool silk of the chestnut waves between his fingers.

Lani shrugged. "Colonisers have always tried to impart their ways on the islands. Some things we take and use, others we dismiss. This style of architecture is popular across much of the Pacific. If you pay attention, you will notice the native symbols engraved in the balustrades on both levels. However, the majority of the common areas are open, supported by pillars. This is how the *fale*, or homes, of our people are designed. Our official buildings are merely a representation of our heritage."

"Is this where you grew up?"

Stella's inquiry shook something loose in Aleki. He snorted indelicately. "No, little star. My brother and I did spend many hours running around the verandah here, but we moved between the other residences for most of my childhood. This is where important things happen, and important matters are of no concern to children. When I became a man at twenty I was gifted one of the parcels of land under the royal holdings, and built my own house there."

"Yours is a very different style, " Stella observed, and Aleki bit back a smile.

"That is not by accident." After years of being stuck in dark wooden rooms brimming with tradition, he had purposefully designed his home to reflect light and space. 'Neo-Moorish Minimalism', the architect had called it.

"I like yours better." Heat trickled through him as Stella's lips curved upwards in a cheeky smile. If anything could distract him from his father's ire, it was those lips. Full and lush, painted a pretty pink. As he watched, her tongue flicked out and wet them, leaving a glistening sheen behind that he longed to sample. Desire buzzed in his ears, filling his head, pulsing low in his groin. Craving the sensation of his mouth on hers, he leaned forward, eyes locked on his target.

Just a taste.

"Your Highness!" The bite in Lani's tone warned him this might not be the first time she'd spoken.

"My liege?" The spell broken, he leaned back against

the smooth leather of the seat, dragging his eyes from the temptation of heaven that sat not a foot from him.

Lani flushed at the hated nickname. "The car has stopped."

"So it has." He looked back at Stella, his stomach knotting at the wariness he saw as she studied him.

The door opened and a shaft of light cut across Stella's face as the sun filtered into the dark interior. It picked out the gold in her hair and the emerald fire in the eye it touched. Responsibility settled itself heavily on Aleki's shoulders as he considered for the first time how much she was giving up to help him live his life the way he wanted. Reaching out, he enfolded her hand in his, stroking his thumb lightly across the veins inside her wrist.

"Everything will be okay," he assured her. "I'll look after you."

"I'll look after myself, thank you very much," Stella replied lightly. "But you can help, if you like."

Aleki felt his face break into a grin.

"As you wish," he replied gently. "Now, let's go see a king about a wedding."

Alighting from the car, he turned to help Stella out, and almost missed the intake of breath from the staff lined up to greet them.

Not a great start.

Part of it was the unfamiliar presence of a woman beside him, he knew that. But some of it was how that woman looked. Bringing a *palagi* woman inside the gates was not without significance, and only time would tell whether or not it would be received well. If nothing else, she looked the part of a visiting princess. Her dress had maintained its crispness on the drive, and her black belt and matching flats were stylish but sensible.

Fighting his nerves, he offered his arm and was gratified when she accepted it. Lani and Andreas fell in behind them as he led the group across the paved driveway and up the wide wooden steps, nodding at the staff who bowed their heads in deference at his passing. Once inside, his entourage peeled off, leaving the two of them to proceed ahead to the Great Hall, where he knew instinctively his father would be waiting. King Tama was a fan of the power move.

Sure enough, the spacious room was empty, save for the wide tapa mat on the floor in front of the raised platform where his father lolled on the carved wooden throne that symbolised Aleki's future.

"Come, my son."

Aleki fought a smirk at the dramatics. He'd seen his father three days ago, yet here he was acting as though he was returning from war. Were it not for the importance of the woman beside him and all she represented, he would have let his amusement bloom on his face. But that would not help him now.

Approaching the dais, Stella's hand still firmly grasped in his, Aleki bowed his head.

"May I present Miss Stella Warren, my guest from New Zealand. Miss Warren, His Majesty King Tama of Avali, my father."

Wrestling her hand from his, Stella curtseyed. Impressively, for someone unfamiliar with the custom. "It is an honour, Your Majesty."

"The pleasure is mine, Miss Warren," the king lied smoothly. "Please, make yourselves comfortable."

Aleki settled himself cross-legged on the tapa cloth and was joined by Stella after a moment's hesitation. The coolness of the hardwood floors seeped through the mat.

Comfortable, it was not, but that was the nature of these games they played.

"Might I ask that we speak in English, Father? Stella has not yet mastered our language."

"Leai." King Tama's response was swift.

"What is it you wish to achieve?" the king continued in his native tongue. "You commandeer my plane to bring home a tryst? Are you trying to prove to your people that you are nothing more than a boy, ruled by his hormones?"

Cold seeped through Aleki, icy fingers reaching through his stomach and twining up his torso. Fear of letting down his people gripped at his heart, squeezing until his chest felt like it might explode.

"It is not like that, Father. I would never disrespect the subjects of Avali by bringing a woman I was not serious about to our shores."

King Tama snorted, curling the lips under his neatly trimmed mustache in a sneer. "You cannot be serious about this woman, son. Bringing her here will do nothing but cause rumours and unease amongst our people. Send her home, and I will find you a nice Avali girl if you wish to settle down."

Aleki steeled himself. "I wish to settle down with Stella, Your Majesty. She has agreed to be my wife."

The king pierced Aleki with his glare as the air around him stilled. Every thread on his graphite suit seemed to hover as the air around him vibrated with barely suppressed rage.

"You have not proposed marriage to this woman."

Aleki averted his eyes, focusing on the tips of his shoes and the aged tapa beneath them.

"I have."

"You foolish boy," the king exploded, his voice soaring to

the rafters of the cavernous hall. "How dare you bring this woman here, making her promises you can not hope to keep! Do you care nothing for your people? You can not trifle with them in this way. You have a responsibility to the crown of Avali. If you wish to marry, you will marry the daughter of a chief and ensure our bloodline is strong. This woman has no place here, in our family, in our culture. She knows nothing of what it means to be an Esera! And you, my son, where is your judgement? All of your life, I have raised you to put the needs of your people first. I have overlooked your indiscretions overseas because they have not interfered with your role here. But this is unacceptable. The people of Avali will not accept a white woman on their throne. To say nothing of what might happen if she were to produce an heir."

Aleki winced, and the air shifted.

"You stupid boy." Realisation and disappointment weighted each of his father's quiet words, sending them sinking heavily to the pit of Aleki's stomach like stones. "Take your whore and get out."

SIX

The tiles were cool under Stella's feet as she padded barefoot to the king sized bed and flopped on it with all the grace of an injured sea lion. A groan that started in her toes soared up to the high wooden rafters, filling the air with the sound of her distress. After their disastrous meeting with the king, Aleki had hustled her back into the limo and swept her back to his residence in dreadful silence. The kind of silence that hung heavy in the air, buffeting away all pretense of lightness. Not wanting to push, Stella had remained silent too, even though her gut was screaming to reach out and touch him, to offer him solace or at least support while he struggled with the turmoil their visit inside the gates had unleashed. She hadn't though. She'd never seen a man less likely to appreciate it. So they'd sat, side by side, in stony silence until Andreas had pulled to a halt, and then Aleki had leapt from the car as if it were on fire and retreated into the depths of the house without a backwards glance.

She rolled over onto her back, pressing her cheek

against the brightly patterned quilt in traditional Avali designs. She was in the same room she'd stayed in for Mae and Luke's wedding, and there was something soothing about a touch of familiarity right now, with everything else in her world so up in the air.

Someone rapped at the door and Stella forced herself into a sitting position for decorum's sake.

"Come in."

"Ms Warren?" Lani poked her head around the dark wooden door. "I have some documents from His Highness for you."

"That sounds extremely boring, Lani. Come on in."

"Boring gets things done, Ms Warren."

"I hear you there. Water?" Stella gestured to the large jug and drinking glasses set up on a low table by the doors to the balcony. A vase of lavender roses sat beside the water jug, looking oddly out of place in the tropical surroundings.

"No thank you, ma'am."

"Lani, I'm going to be here for the next two weeks at a minimum. Can you call me Stella? Please," she added when the other woman hesitated. "It would mean a lot to me."

"If that is what you would like, I would be happy to do so."

Stella smiled, a little jump of success flourishing in her chest. "Not the enthusiasm I'd hoped for, but I appreciate it anyway. Now, what dull paperwork have you brought for me?"

"There are the standard non-disclosure agreements, of course. Some files with personal details to keep on record, a list of different charities His Highness supports, an upcoming itinerary of his events."

"I see. Will any of these upcoming events have King Tama present?"

Lani's lips pressed into a thin line as she nodded once in acknowledgement.

"That should be fun." Stella gestured to the folders in Lani's arms. "May I?"

She flicked through the papers requesting copies of her birth certificate and general information-gathering questions. Despite the somewhat tedious nature of the forms, Stella's admiration grew as she took in the quality of the timelines, the colour coding, the font choices.

"Did you prepare this paperwork, Lani?"

"I prepared all the internal paperwork. Some documents have been prepared by Prince Aleki's personal legal team. He uses a separate one to the rest of the royal family."

"You're a woman of many talents." Stella smiled up at Lani, who was still standing stiffly, with her hands behind her back. "Perhaps I've chosen the wrong Avalian to marry."

Lani finally looked at her, the skin around her deep brown eyes crinkling as she grinned. "While I appreciate the compliment, Stella, my girlfriend may not. She would fight you for me, and she would win. You and I will have to put our passion for each other's organisational talents aside and simply focus on running the country for His Highness."

"Just one country, though, Lani? We could rule the world."

"I'll think about it."

"That's my girl." Stella chuckled, opening a white folder with the crest of Avali imprinted on it in red. The heading of the first page jumped out at her in bold black type.

Matrimonial Contract between His Highness Prince Aleki Esera of Avali and Stella Rose Warren.

Mother effer. He'd sent this to her with the other paperwork regarding her shoe size and blood type? A chill spread through her. *Even friends don't treat each other like this.*

"Lani?"

"Stella?"

"Could you please locate Aleki and tell him I'd like to speak to him immediately?"

"I'm not sure he's-"

"Immediately. Please." Her voice was as icy as her blood.

"Certainly." From her peripherals, she saw the other woman incline her head before departing.

Stella read through the contract as dispassionately as she could, fighting down the voices of the demons that slid through her mind. Whispers that she wasn't good enough, that she wasn't worth talking to. That her desires were irrelevant because a man had already decided what she was worth.

To-Do List. Set clear expectations. Retain own lawyer. Question clause 6.

"Stella?"

She looked up. Aleki leaned against the open door frame of her bedroom, his arms folded across his chest. Gone was the suit and tie, the coiffed hair. He wore a plain grey tee that hugged the olive skin of his biceps. Black workout shorts were slung low on his hips and his hair fell forward against his forehead, curling slightly from sweat.

Fire licked through the ice, and Stella struggled to hold onto the chill, any semblance of coolness in the way she spoke.

"You were busy?"

"I was boxing. It helps." He looked away, gesturing vaguely. "You know, with my father. Most of our discussions end with me taking my frustrations out on the bag."

"Are you frustrated with him or me?"

Dark eyes shot up to meet hers. "Him, *fafine aulelei*. Only him. And perhaps myself a little."

She chose her words carefully. "I'm also a little frustrated with you."

"Because?"

Stella narrowed her eyes at him and let the silence swell.

Aleki closed his eyes and ran one big hand over his jaw. "Because I'm a dick." It wasn't a question.

"And why are you a dick, Aleki?"

"Because I didn't stand up for you in front of my dad. I let him speak Avalian. I didn't answer in English so you could follow along. And I ignored you on the way home."

"A decent deduction. You also let him call me a whore."

Aleki winced. "I was kind of hoping you'd forgotten what *talitane* meant."

"And then there's this." Stella indicated the contract spread over the bedspread.

Aleki levered himself off the doorframe and approached the bed. Stella held her breath as he flopped next to her on the bed, lest the smell of clean, male sweat combined with the visuals of his long brown limbs cause her ovaries to spontaneously combust. Despite the topic of their conversation, this was the most relaxed she'd seen Aleki since she'd first turned up on his doorstep two months ago. It was evident in his clothes, but also in the way he spoke - less formal, more contractions. The Aleki from university was still hidden under the suits and ceremony, and these small glimpses of him were doing nothing to dull her attraction. If she'd caught him fresh from boxing training the day she'd arrived in Avali she'd probably have jumped him in the foyer.

"Our contract? That's what you're upset about, little star?"

"This is a contract for our marriage, Aleki. An agreement between two people."

"Mmm. So it is." His voice was lower, gravelly. She glanced up from the paperwork to find his dark eyes locked on hers.

"So," she responded, stumbling over a small hitch in her breath. "We're supposed to be a team now. It would be appropriate for you to present it to me for consideration. Not have it delivered with a pile of other meaningless correspondence. It feels," she hesitated slightly, "impersonal."

"And you would like our marriage to be personal?"

"I would like our marriage to be respectful. We haven't discussed the details yet, whether it will be a union in name only, or certain requirements either of us may have, but I would like to think that we respect each other enough to decide these between us. Not have them discussed around a conference table by a bunch of lawyers."

"Look at the back page."

"The back page?" Stella reclined next to Aleki and flipped through the drab pages of legalese until a bright yellow handwritten Post-It caught her eye by the witness section.

You'll be lucky if she even agrees to marry your dumb arse. -L.

"Luke had something to do with this?"

"His brother drafted it. He's a solicitor. It's a boilerplate prenup, with a few additions thrown in for the baby and royalty factors. But yes. I asked him to draft something after I booked my flight to see you in Wellington. I had no idea what you would say, if you'd agree to see me, let alone marry me. I wanted you to know you had options to ensure the best life possible for you and the baby. And I wanted you to be protected even if you didn't want me involved. But you're right. These factors are in cases of a marriage in name only." Quicker than she would have expected, Aleki claimed the contract from her hands and repositioned himself with his head on her lap, looking up at the papers in his hands.

"So we should negotiate?"

"There will be no negotiation, little star. Not through lawyers at least." He ripped the contract in half.

Confusion muddied Stella's thoughts.

"What?"

"You agreed to marry me, Stella. Without seeing this contract, without those discussions, without any requirements. That nullifies the need for any documentation. This will not be a marriage in name only. You will say my name, and often, because I will be your husband. You will be my wife, and I will call your name to the heavens. Our marriage might be convenient, and we may not love each other, but we have acquiesced to spend the rest of our lives together. This is not the kind of agreement that is sealed with a contract."

Her breath caught.

"How, um, how will it be sealed?"

"I think you know, Stella." Aleki turned and pressed his face against her stomach, his breath warm against the fabric pressed to her skin.

The heat spread through Stella's body, tunnelling down in a tight coil towards her centre. Shifting slightly, she pressed her thighs together, trying to ease the growing ache between them.

Aleki looked up, his eyes fixing on her, hot and dark. Hungry.

"Am I making you uncomfortable, little star?"

"No." Her breath hitched on the word, wholly unconvincing even to her own ears.

"No?" Aleki leaned forward and nudged at the buttons marching up her dress with his nose. "Perhaps a little more fresh air would settle you." One hand reached up to toy with the button at her waist.

"The windows are open." Need threaded through her voice, her attention too focused on where his hand met her dress to modulate it.

"So they are." He slipped the button free, and Stella felt his large hand like a brand against her stomach as he slid under the fabric of her dress to stroke her skin.

"So soft, *fafine aulelei*. Tell me, are you still upset with me?"

Aleki's fingers rose higher, tracing patterns up her ribcage and Stella forgot how to breathe.

"Gurngh," she managed, moving just a *little*, because he was *almost there* and really, what was a relationship without teamwork?

His talented fingers divested another button from the confines of its hole and the fabric of her dress gaped open across her torso, any modesty she had left protected now only by the remaining button over her chest.

Aleki's thumb skimmed the underside of her breast, a delicious friction against the lace of her bra and she watched, mesmerised, as he bent his dark head to her exposed midriff. The hot, sweet stripe of his tongue glided up towards her aching breasts, and Stella lost all patience entirely and ripped open the final button, spreading the lapels of her dress wide and clutching at the silky strands of Aleki's hair.

"Don't stop."

A rough chuckle tickled against her sternum.

"I have no intention of stopping, little star."

Soft kisses peppered the delicate skin of her breasts, moving closer and closer to - *there*.

The liquid heat of Aleki's mouth closed around her nipple and Stella dizzied from the combination of relief and gratitude. He tugged at the tip with his lips, his clever fingers reaching up to pluck at its twin.

"Oh God, yes, like that." Stella arched up, pushing herself forward into his hands, his mouth.

He sucked deeper, his tongue lapping at her nipple and sparks shot through Stella, crackling along her skin and settling between her legs.

"Does that feel good, *fafine aulelei*?"

"Stop talking!"

A warm puff of air sailed across the tender tip of her breast, followed quickly by the rasp of Aleki's jaw as he nuzzled the delicate curve.

"You are so used to being in control, Stella. It's time to relax and let your man take care of you."

Soft teasing bites alternated with gentle licks as Aleki transferred his attention to her other nipple. The rhythm of the soothe-and-scrape dulled her hearing into a heavy throb of lust, narrowing the entirety of her world focus to his mouth and the magical things he was doing to her. She was so focused on his mouth she nearly missed the glide of his hand up her thigh until he was squeezing the curve of her hip with an intensity that might have hurt if she wasn't riding a Keith-Richards-level high of pure lust.

Aleki's fingers flexed again, as hot as a brand, finally pulling some of her attention from the miracle of his mouth, which he conveniently raised to plead with her in a pleasingly ragged voice.

"Can I touch you?"

"Jesus Fucking Christ, yes." Stella squirmed, seeking his fingers, and sagged back against the lush coverlet with a whimper of relief as his thumb dragged slowly up the damp fabric of her underwear.

"Little star, if you're going to say any man's name while my hand is in your pants, you need to make sure it's mine."

His thumb circled the bundle of nerves, firm and unforgiving, flooding her with pleasure that fanned out, up her arms, down to her toes, behind her eyelids.

The swell of pressure built, climbing higher and higher with each delicious press of his fingers, the hot, wet glory of his tongue against her neck and the whisper in her ear.

"*O outou o a'u.* You're mine. You're mine."

Aleki slid one finger inside her, then a second, filling her and rubbing her and whispering his claim and Stella fisted her hand in the cover and forgot about everything else in the world.

"Open your eyes, little star." He met her gaze, his stare devastating, intensity pouring off him in waves. Press, delve, rub.

Oh shit, oh shit, so good.

"Mine."

And her world exploded.

ALEKI LAY in a patch of warm sunlight and thought about Bosnian war crimes. When he was no longer in danger of coming in his pants, he glanced over at Stella. The top of her dress was still open, the bottom hiked up around her hips and a sliver of cream lace on display over the curve of her thigh. He hadn't even caught a peek of her underwear earlier. Her eyes were closed and her lush mouth curved in a beatific smile. The sight of his woman sated by his hand caused a thud of possession to pound in Aleki's chest like a deep, politically incorrect drum. Tension had ridden him like an unbridled stallion since the meeting with his father. A session in the gym had helped, but it was no match for Stella. As soon as he'd seen her lolling on her bed, his heart had lightened. She was worth every harsh word from the king, and more, because she had agreed to marry him and have his baby. And now, lying in the mid-afternoon light with the echoes of her cries still ringing in his ears, any residual anxiety had evaporated completely.

"So we're getting married."

It wasn't a question, but he answered anyway.

"We are."

"Properly married."

"As married as two people can be."

"No contracts."

"None, little star. It was a mistake to have one drafted. I wasn't sure if you'd take me without guarantees."

"But the king still hates me."

Unease jackknifed through Aleki. "He doesn't hate you. He is disappointed in me. In my actions, and what it means for our people."

"What does it mean for your people?"

Aleki shrugged, discomfort prickling over his skin.

"Some diplomatic relationships may become strained. There was talk last year of whether the Tongan princess and I would make a good match."

"You were dating that hot French Formula One driver last year."

"Little star." He didn't even try to hide his delight. "Have you been keeping tabs on me?"

One smooth shoulder rose slightly but Aleki had the distinct impression that if Stella Warren was the kind of woman who blushed, she would be doing so now.

"It was in a magazine when I was in line at the supermarket. Honestly, Aleki," she cracked one eye open and met his gaze. "I know you were on the Riviera, but you should still consider wearing something to swim in. The entire world could live happily without ever seeing your penis."

"Would you live happily without ever seeing my penis?"

"Sure. Aesthetics are worthless. As long as it keeps me happy through the sense of touch -" Stella broke off mid-sentence as Aleki threw a few pages of their ripped contract at her.

The tinkle of her laughter rang in his ears and he smiled at the ceiling.

"Will she be terribly disappointed?"

"Who?"

"The Tongan princess."

"She ought to. If she's read the same magazine as you, she'll know exactly what she's missing out on."

"Aleki."

He heaved a sigh. "I will not lie to you, little star. My father has made his expectations for me clear. It is the king's duty to set an example for his people. The Riviera photos were not my finest moment and I was given a significant talking-to about my behaviour. I will be king one day, and it is important to the *mana* of my people that I conduct myself appropriately. Marriage and children is very much a part of that. Indulging in those with an outsider to our Pacific culture will raise eyebrows, but the important thing is that we set a clear example of how to treat each other and our children well. Additionally, I will need to manage any concerns our union raises with our neighbouring islands. I have not yet proven myself worthy to lead my people, but I hope to change that soon."

Stella's threaded her fingertips through his hair, applying enough pressure to set his nerve endings alight with pleasure.

"You will be an incredible king, Aleki."

"I can only hope." He shifted and pulled out a small stack of crumpled paperwork from underneath him.

"What is all of this, *fafine aulelei*? We have been engaged all of three hours, and you have a veritable library of administration here."

"Those are my lists and charts and forms. Lani made them for me and I love her passionately for it. I will marry her once you die and we will reign together."

"Good luck getting past her girlfriend." Aleki flipped through several pages until he found an easy looking form. "Okay. Height?"

"What?"

"We're filling these out now. If Lani is happy, we are all happy. And sometimes when she's in a good mood, she brings in *panipopo* from home, and that makes me happier still. What's your height?"

"Five foot eight."

"Weight?"

"Bugger off. I'm not telling you, and even if I did, the fact that I'm eight weeks pregnant means that it's going to change rapidly."

"A fair point." He wrote an answer in the space regardless. *Perfect*.

"Colours that suit your skin tone?"

"Black, white, cream."

Aleki looked up. Stella's eyes were closed again and she

wiggled her red-tipped toes as she stretched her legs out towards the end of the bed.

"Stella," he replied patiently. "You look fantastic in many colours."

"How do you know?" She kicked each leg gently. "You haven't seen me in anything else since I was eighteen."

Aleki hesitated, his mind running back through each occasion since she'd arrived for Luke and Mae's wedding. She was right.

"You don't wear colours?"

"Nope. I'm busy and it's too much hard work, trying to match things and buy fashionable colours each season. Black and neutrals work for me."

"What about at weddings?" Genuine curiosity piqued his voice. The 'hot French Formula One driver' had spent a ridiculous amount of his money on clothes in Monaco that made her look like an oversized parrot. So had the professor, the pilot and the hedge fund manager that had come before her in various cities of their own.

"I have three identical dresses for working weddings. One in pink, one in navy and one in green. I rotate depending on what the colour scheme and bridesmaid dresses are for each event."

"Shoes?"

"Nude or black."

"Nails?"

"Nude or red."

Aleki stared at her. After several beats, she opened her eyes and turned her head to look at him.

"Why are you staring at me?"

Noise stopped. There was nothing else, just the gleam of her green eyes, the caramel-chocolate swirl of her hair, the tanned skin and the white and black and cream of his future wife laid out on traditional Avali fabric in his home.

He answered honestly.

"Because you are amazing."

And Stella Warren, who was not the kind of woman who blushed, blushed.

SEVEN

"Sir?"

Aleki glanced up from the stack of documents he was reviewing. Orange streaks of light filtered into his office from the sky outside, alerting him to how much time had passed since he had sat down at his desk.

"Ah, Lani. Do you think we might be able to schedule a call with the Samoan trade minister tomorrow? I've got some questions regarding their export routes."

"Aleki." Her tone was firm. "What are you doing?"

Puzzlement furrowed his brow. Lani only ever called him by his first name when she was extremely pissed off.

Did I forget her birthday? No, that's just before Christmas.

"Is there... that is... was I supposed to do something?"

"Yes, you idiot." Aleki flinched. She was not happy at all. No *panipopo* for him in the near future. "You've got a beautiful woman apparently ready to saddle herself to you for life, and so far all you've done is take her to your father's for a telling-off, send her that ridiculous contract and lock yourself in your office through dinner on her first night here.

You were supposed to make her feel welcome, but you've done as good a job of that as you have of keeping your desk under control."

Aleki looked around the papers strewn over his desk. Every morning when he arrived in the office they were stacked neatly, colour coded for urgency, and each night it looked as if it had survived a paper-based blizzard.

"Did Stella eat?"

"No. She claims she's not feeling well." Lani's reproach was palpable, and the sting of it settled in his chest.

"You are right." Aleki met his assistant's gaze head on. "I have been distracted by this deal. But it is no excuse to neglect my responsibilities elsewhere. Can you please rearrange my calendar for the next week to ensure that my afternoons and evenings are free?"

Lani nodded once, silently assessing him as he rose and approached the doorway. He patted her arm once on the way past her. "You're a good friend, Lani. Thank you."

After a quick stop in the kitchen, he made his way to the top of the stairs and knocked on Stella's door. His house was modest by royal standards, even in the islands. There were only four bedrooms on the upper level, including the master suite, all currently closed off behind their doors.

From behind the wood, a groan rumbled.

"Come in."

Holding the tray carefully in one hand, he turned the knob and maneuvered into the darkened room. The curtains were pulled against the island sunset, the only light coming from a small lamp on one of the polished concrete bedside tables. Stella was curled up under the blue and black patterned coverlet, her hair caught up in a messy ponytail. She eyed him suspiciously as he crossed towards her.

"How are you feeling?" He settled the tray on the bedside table furthest from her and settled himself on the bed, over the covers.

"Terrible." Her narrowed eyes shone up at him from a cosy cocoon of pillows. "What idiot named it 'morning sickness' when it lasts all frigging day?"

Aleki huffed out a gentle laugh even as guilt bit under his skin. He should have checked on her earlier. "You should take it up with the World Health Organization."

"I intend to." She snuggled deeper into her nest. "How was the rest of your day?"

"Busy. I should not have left you alone though. That was thoughtless of me."

A small shrug. "You're an important guy. I imagine you have more important things to do than watch me lie around moaning."

He growled, the sound pulled out of him at her words despite his best intentions. "Oh, little star. You could not be more wrong. Lying in bed watching you as you moan would be the most spectacular way to spend a day."

Humour glinted in her eyes as she peeked up at him, a reluctant smile tugging at the side of her full lips.

"You are such a dork."

"Come," Aleki patted the padded headboard. "Sit up. Let a dork feed you."

Stella hefted herself upwards, plumping the pillows behind her as she rearranged herself in a seated position. She snagged one strap of her black tank as it slipped down her shoulders and hooked it back into place with her thumb. Aleki almost groaned aloud at the temptation.

"You may present your offerings."

"For your consideration, ma'am. Firstly, we have the egg and cheese toastie. Fully cooked egg to prevent any salmonella concerns, real butter used to toast each side, a protein-packed extravaganza. Next," Aleki rotated the large plate so Stella could see the items on it in more detail. "Taro chips. Salty and delicious, just like you." She rolled her eyes. "And finally, banana bread, baked fresh this morning using bananas from our own garden, ."

He held the tray in the perfect imitation of an infomercial presenter while Stella gazed upon the riches of his kitchen.

"Toastie," she declared firmly, accepting the sandwich as he handed it over, a recycled paper napkin wrapped around it to prevent the burning of her fingers.

"Excellent choice, ma'am. And to drink? Your options are water or a vanilla milkshake."

"Milkshake!" Stella bounced happily on the bed, her earlier lethargy gone. She accepted the frosty aluminum vessel from him and sucked half of it down through the metal straw immediately.

Her sigh was almost sexual. "God that's good. When we're married, you will be Chief Milkshake Maker. I'll have Luke add it to the contract."

"It would be my honour." Aleki scooped up a handful of taro chips and crunched into one. "So, pregnancy really is that terrible?"

"It's not fun. I'm sure the flight has something to do with it as well, but I'm exhausted and nauseous. I always assumed I'd be one of those glowing pregnant women who swanned about in elegant kaftans when I decided to have children, but I feel more like Oscar the Grouch with narcolepsy."

Aleki snorted gently. "You've never struck me as the trashcan type."

Stella shrugged as she bit off the corner of her toasted

sandwich. "How the mighty have fallen, huh?" The question was mumbled around a mouthful of egg and cheese.

They fell silent, while they ate, the air punctuated with the munching of chips and toasted bread. Without talking, they shared the banana bread, each picking small chunks off and licking the moist cake crumbs off their fingertips.

"Aleki?" Stella broke the quiet, stabbing her straw into the last centimetres of her shake.

"Hmmm?"

"Why did you leave me in Wellington?"

The easy calm that had been stealing over Aleki halted in his chest, pulling taut throughout his stomach. Stella avoided looking at him, her gaze fixed on the foam at the bottom of her cup.

He sighed deeply. "I shouldn't have done that." He let his mind drift back to the first night he'd been with Stella.

"I liked you from the first time we met. Do you remember?"

She nodded slightly. "Mae dragged me down to the field under the cable car to meet her new boyfriend. You guys were chucking a rugby ball around down there." She sniggered. "I told her Luke better be passing his law classes because he couldn't pass the ball for shit."

Aleki's laugh rumbled low in his chest. "You were wearing a green scarf and the wind kept picking it up and whipping it around your face. We all went to the pub for dinner that night. You ate the biggest burger they had on the menu and then the two of you beat us at pool."

"It's probably a good thing you've taken up boxing actually," Stella mused lightly, still staring down into the milky abyss. "Your ball skills leave a lot to be desired."

"Much more of that mouth missy, and you won't see my ball skills for a month."

She snorted, but he continued. "After that, you were everywhere. I took that final Commerce paper because I had a free space in my timetable and you were doing it. Then you kissed me at games night after our exam and it was like I was standing on the edge of a cliff. I could stay where I was and I'd be safe, or I could fall over the edge and be lost. And I thought 'bugger it' and jumped."

"You did?"

"I did." Aleki ran a hand through his hair. "And then my dad called. He wanted to see how my last exam had gone. I told him it was fine, but I was thinking of staying another year and finishing my degree in New Zealand. Do you know how much it costs for international students at New Zealand universities?" He glanced over at Stella who shook her head mutely, still fixated on her shake. "It's a lot. There's a fund here on the island. Everyone contributes what they can and scholarship recipients get to study over-seas. But only for a year, unless the subject isn't offered here in Avali."

"And you wanted to stay longer?"

"I mentioned it. My dad didn't take it well. He laid down an ultimatum. I could stay and finish my degree in New Zealand but there wouldn't be a place for me here in governance. So I left."

A heavy exhale rang out from next to him.

"Without a goodbye?"

"Stella." Aleki reached out and clasped the hand holding her straw, wrapping her chilled fingers in his. "You were not the kind of girl a boy relishes saying goodbye to. I was afraid that if I talked to you again, kissed you, I would lose all reason and stay. My people needed me. But more than that, I needed them. I needed to prove that their money and their faith in me had not been wasted."

"Yes," Stella's full lips twisted wrly. "It's such a terrible shame to have your faith in someone wasted."

He removed the shake from her fingers, placing it on the bedside table. A drop of condensation ran down the side, pooling on the polished concrete like a tear.

"Did you hate me after?"

"Yes." Her quiet candor cut through him. "A little for the leaving, but mostly for the lying. I went to the clinic for a checkup after you left and saw you on a magazine cover in the waiting room. That's when I realised who you were. It felt like everything we'd been through, all of the late nights, the cram sessions, the paella and chocolate buffets in the library, everything had been tainted. I didn't put a lot of emphasis on the fact that I lost my virginity that night, but the fact that I'd lost it to someone who I'd never really known made me bitter. It took a long time for that wound to heal."

"But it did?"

Stella shrugged and snuggled back down so her head nestled back on the pillow. Her voice grew heavy with fatigue.

"Mostly. I had quite a few one night stands after that. I left while they were sleeping, just like you had done to me. I never called them back or gave them another chance. Giving someone else the opportunity to hurt me seemed like madness. There were some nice guys, some good times. But none of them have lasted. I tell myself it's this business, the hours. But it's not."

Regret tore through Aleki at the resignation in Stella's sleep-leaden tone. He'd been a scared young man - barely more than a child - when he'd left her. He'd never considered that his actions might have affected Stella past the walk of shame home and a simmering resentment for him.

"Is that why you don't believe in love?" The question slipped out unbidden.

She huffed out a sardonic laugh, even as her eyes drifted closed. "I believe in love just fine. I see it every day in my work. But it's not in my future."

"And that's why you agreed to marry me?"

"Yeah." Her soft lips curled in a small smile. "My child deserves a father who loves it more than anything. You can be that. If you couldn't, I wouldn't be here."

Aleki's gut tightened as she spoke. *Nothing but a baby daddy.* Well, he couldn't fault her honesty. She was following the terms of their agreement to the letter. Stella had never been much for sentimentality. He reached out and stroked several escaped strands from her ponytail back off her forehead. The cool tresses felt at odds with the warmth of her brow, and he kept stroking, light little repetitions, as her breathing grew heavy and even.

When he was sure she was asleep, he rolled to the side of the bed and kicked off his shoes. His shirt and pants followed, and he slipped beneath the crisp cotton of the coverlet wearing only his boxer briefs. Reaching out, he captured one of her lax hands in his and linked their fingers together as he closed his eyes. He couldn't erase the mistrust he'd caused the mother of his child in the past, but he could make damn sure she woke up to find him there in the morning.

STELLA LOVED A GREAT MANY THINGS. But nothing compared to the languid joy she felt when it came to waking up slowly in clean sheets and sunlight. Her Wellington apartment faced the east and with a lack of neighbours on that side, she rarely pulled her bedroom blinds, just so she could wake up like this - soft and warm on her stomach, nestled in thread counts higher than her credit card limit. The sticky weight of slumber loosened its hold as she turned her face towards the light, little pinpricks of gold settling behind her closed lids like a torch under blankets.

Burrowing her cheek deeper into the plush pillow, she stretched out a little. Just enough to stir her blood, send a few light endorphins skittering through her blood. Like every morning, she wiggled her toes while she ran through her To-Do List for the day.

And... nothing.

Stella frowned, scanning back in her mind for a reminder of what she had on today, but her ever-present internal catalogue of tasks remained stubbornly blank. She stretched again, arching her back this time and her hip grazed against something firm. She moved once more, rubbing her hip against the foreign entity even as she registered a muffled noise beside her.

Eyes flying open, she jerked up into a sitting position.

"Stella?"

"Aleki?" She glanced around the room quickly as recollection struck, then returned her gaze to him. It was a mistake.

Aleki Esera was stunning in suits, gorgeous in gym gear and fantasy-fuel in traditional Avalian garb. She'd Googled it. But in bed?

Breathtaking.

His short dark hair tufted up in soft-looking peaks, unencumbered by product. Stubble coated his square jaw and his eyes, the colour of rich milk chocolate, swam with a drowsy tenderness that made her want nothing more than to snuggle into the crook of his arm and inhale him. And his body... dear God, his body.

Bronzed skin for miles, taut over the planes and ridges of his torso and arms. A sprinkling of dark hair covered his chest and narrowed as it traveled down beneath the brightly coloured quilt to the lap she'd been grinding her hip against. Flat brown nipples peeked out from the crisp curls. Dizziness hit Stella like a brick as she flashed back to tugging on one with her teeth the night of Mae and Luke's wedding while Aleki pinned her against the door to her room with her dress bunched around her waist and his hands firm on her arse.

"*Fafine aulelei?*" Aleki's voice ripped her from her lust-soaked memory. "Are you alright?"

"I...um...yes." Except she wasn't because she was stuttering like a fool and the memory fireworks were still going on behind her eyelids, image after filthy image of fevered debauchery. She shook her head.

Be gone, mental sex memior!

"Why are you here?"

Aleki raised one thick eyebrow. "We are engaged."

"Yes." Stella dragged the word out slowly. "But we're engaged because we're having a baby. The baby isn't here yet and won't be for months."

"You wish to cease all contact until you've finished delivering?" She could hear the teasing tone under the mock-seriousness.

"I'm just surprised, that's all. I've never woken up next to you. It's strange."

Aleki's mouth pursed, unhappiness clear in the downward tilt of his lips.

"Perhaps you should move into my room."

Stella's breath caught in her chest, a quick skip of hope that was doused as soon as he spoke again.

"It would be the most convenient solution for our circumstances."

The meaning of his statement landed squarely on her silly notions. *It's not you he wants. It's your body.*

"I don't think that's a good idea. Maybe once we're married. Or even when the baby arrives. Right now I still need my own space."

Aleki's brow furrowed as she spoke, an adorable crease that she smoothed out with her thumb. The sun-warmed velvet of his skin was nothing but temptation and Stella almost groaned for holding back the need that twisted through her to take his lips with her own. But she'd already shown too much of herself last night. The fact that he hadn't bolted from her bed before the sun rose was a miracle in itself. Any sign of neediness now outside of the demands of the pregnancy would only be to open herself up to hurt.

"So," she sang brightly, slipping out from under the covers. "What are your plans for today?"

Aleki ran his hand over his unshaven jaw, the light rasp sending electricity shooting straight to her nipples. Stella headed for her suitcase, ignoring the ache and praying he hadn't noticed them tightening under her tank.

"I have a council meeting with all the village leaders this morning. I will inform them of our engagement and take stock of their responses. There may be some resistance to such a sudden announcement, but it will be better to identify any problems now. Are you free this afternoon?"

Stella looked up from her crouched position by her luggage, a bundle of clothes in her arms.

"I arrived yesterday. What could I possibly be doing this afternoon?"

Aleki's smile was sly. "*Fafine aulelei*, for all I know you could have already organised plans for a rally promoting turtle conservation efforts. I would put nothing past you. But as it happens, I do believe Lani has organised some lessons for you to help you learn some of the language and culture of the island."

"She has?" Gratitude flooded Stella. "That's so kind. I started researching the night I found out about the pregnancy, but so many sites just discuss the Pacific Islands in general and each island has such a specific culture. I don't want to get anything wrong." She hesitated slightly, sinking her teeth into her bottom lip as she stared at the future king in her bed. "I don't want to embarrass you."

"Never," Aleki replied blithely, though she noticed the way his eyes slid from hers before he swung out of bed. He strode towards her, sleek and powerful, then ruined the effect entirely by patting her on the shoulder like she was his gereatric aunt.

"Will you meet me in the foyer at two? I'd like to show you something."

Stella nodded mutely, trying to ignore the buzz of nerves vibrating through her from a *goddamned shoulder pat*. Unaffected, Aleki smiled at her cheerfully, and wandered out of the room, naked except for his underwear.

Sitting back on the tiles, Stella concentrated on breathing, dragging air in and holding it for a moment before exhaling.

In and out. In and out. In and out.

She was no stranger to sleepovers, but waking up next to a man wasn't usually fraught with so many expectations. Like meeting later in the day. Moving into their space. *Marrying them and having their baby.*

Stella had assumed that her past experience with

friends of the beneficial variety would be an advantage. Keeping action and emotion separate was child's play for her, but something about Aleki drew down into her and twisted her insides uncomfortably. She'd lied to him last night. Realising Aleki's true identity after their first night of passion had been a shock, but nothing compared to the pain that had sliced through her when she woke to an empty apartment. She'd gone to Mae's, who had cheerily informed her that her lover had left the country before she'd even awoken. Mortification had flooded her, hot and tight, squeezing through her organs and settling heavy in the base of her throat. It was that shame that had prevented her from divulging to Mae the changed nature of her relationship with Aleki. Who wanted to admit that their first time ended with their partner putting an ocean between them? Stella knew well enough what it was like to be a disappointment - her father's face had glowed with evidence of it every time she asked to take gymnastics instead of rugby and he was reminded of the son she would never be. Having Mae and Luke see her painted in that light, even by proxy, was unthinkable.

Keep it together, Warren. Her inner voice bolstered her. *You know how to do this. Sex is for fun and emotions are for animal videos on the Internet. Don't get confused just because you're in it for the long run.*

Her inner pep talk was interrupted by a knock at the door. Lani poked her head in and smiled.

"Stella? His Highness asked that your breakfast be delivered."

Stella scrambled up from the floor, letting her clothes fall in favour of snagging her robe out of her suitcase.

"Of course, Lani. Thank you so much." She belted the thin satin around her waist as the other woman bustled in and set the tray down on the small table in the sitting area. Beyond the glass doors, the lush lawns ran down to the cliffs and the sea glittered like a jewel in the distance. Stella crossed the room and sank one of the low armchairs by the glass-topped table. Her gaze caught on the roses she'd noticed yesterday.

"I love those flowers, Lani. Do they grow well here on the island?"

"Nope." Lani shot a glance at Stella from beneath her strong brows. "Too much humidity. Roses have to be imported."

Stella raised a brow. "Aleki imports roses just for decor?" The extravagance didn't match with his focus on supporting local businesses.

"He does now," Lani grinned, her lips stretching wide around straight, white teeth. "Called me three days ago and insisted on having a standing order set up with a New Zealand supplier."

"Oh?" Stella's curiosity grew. "Which supplier?"

"Aotearoa Roses."

Delight trickled through Stella. "They're wonderful! They supply my friend Bethany. She has a shop down the street from me and I recommend all my clients to her if they haven't selected a florist."

"Fancy that." Lani's smile widened further.

"Yes. Actually, when he was in New Zealand, Aleki asked me who I would suggest for flowers..." Stella's voice drifted off as realisation dawned. The twittering of birdsong outside drifted in through the filmy curtains and swirled around the silence of the room.

Lani reached out and patted her hand gently.

"I'll be back in an hour and we can talk about a programme to go over royal etiquette, alright?"

"Okay," Stella replied quietly. "Thank you Lani."

The other woman left, and Stella looked at the breakfast tray on the table next to the vase of lavender roses. A chia cup, a fresh fruit platter and a pot of what smelt like English Breakfast tea next to a perfect china teacup and saucer. Aleki had sent up the exact breakfast she'd selected every morning they'd eaten together before the wedding. Her heart clenched with an unfamiliar and unwelcome pulse of tenderness.

Shit.

EIGHT

"You're not serious."

Lani laughed over one perfectly undulating shoulder at the horror on Stella's face. "It's tradition," she called over the low pulse of the music.

"How can it be traditional in a country that prides itself on modesty for me to cover myself in oil and dance for a group of strangers?"

Lani chuckled again, the sound echoing up to the high ceiling of the foyer. "Come give it a go and I'll tell you."

Stella took a few dubious steps towards the middle of the floor and let Lani's movements guide her through a simple eight-beat of choreography.

One, two, three, four. One, two, three, four. And again...

Her movements were stilted, awkward compared to the flowing grace of Lani's arms as she reached into the air, twisting her hands in gentle gestures.

"So," the other woman began, reaching out to guide Stella's flailing limbs into softer arches, "the *taualaga* is the final performance at an Avalian wedding or celebration. It is considered the climax of the evening, and none of the elders will leave until it is performed."

"Even if it's performed by a white girl with no sense of rhythm?"

"Especially then. People are going to be looking for a reason to disapprove of you. It's a solo dance, but often the boys will jump in and dance around the performer, calling out and acting in a humorous way. This emphasises the grace of the female dancer and the balance between the honour and respect of the islands and our fun-loving nature."

One, two, three, four. One, two, three, four.

"And the oil?"

Lani shrugged. "We put coconut oil on everything we can. Skin, hair, babies. We use it for cooking, for ceremonies, for cleaning. And not just the oil. The coconut water for drinking, the flesh for eating, the fronds for weaving, the wood for building. Trust me, Stella. If you're going to marry a Pacific Islander, you're going to need to get comfortable with people rubbing oil on you."

"Stop encouraging my future wife to let strangers rub her." Aleki's voice rumbled with amusement through the foyer.

Stella stumbled for a minute, lowering her arms as discomfort blistered across her skin. The foreign movements, the obscure music, the alien clutch of her heart as she took in Aleki's nonchalant posture leaning against one of the pillars, all combined in a rising sense of dread that she was hopelessly unprepared for the reality she had signed up for.

What are you thinking? Marrying a man who will rule a country? A man you can't predict, can't control?

Aleki's eyes narrowed on her face as he pushed off the pillar.

"Are you okay, little star?"

Gulping, she nodded faintly, watching his approach. One thick eyebrow quirked mockingly, and he reached down and claimed a fallen hand.

"Stella looks parched, Lani. Could you possibly fetch her a glass of water?" He waited until his assistant had left the foyer area before speaking again.

"You are learning the *taualaga*?" Another nod. She was like a dashboard dog on a particularly bumpy road. "What an honour. To be able to watch the mother of my child learn the performance of my people." He raised her hand to the air and disentangled his fingers from hers. "Show me?"

"I'm not good." Her voice was small, uncertain.

Aleki shrugged, the casual rise and fall of his shoulders at odds with the intensity in his brown eyes. "Practice improves everything. But the spirit of the dance, that comes from here." He dragged a knuckle down her sternum as her breath caught in her chest, twisting tight under the brush of his finger. "And in here, you are as good as anyone I have ever met."

"I don't think that's true."

"I once saw you punch a white supremist on the steps of your Parliment, so you'll have to forgive me if I disagree. Now," he waggled his eyebrows suggestively, "show me what you've got."

Blushing, both at the instruction and the reminder of one of her more physical altercations with the far right in uni, Stella started moving again, swaying her hips gently as she touched her middle fingers to her thumbs and twirled her wrists in a gauche approximation of Lani's chore-ography.

Aleki stepped back, a grin powerful enough to light the room spreading across his gorgeous face as he clapped his hands firmly and began to move. Even in tight grey pants and a white shirt, his hips surged beyond the expected restraints of his clothing, rolling and swaying with a natural cadence born of both heritage and habit. He bent his knees, his pelvis swinging lower as he extended his arms towards her as though in worship.

Stella turned in the slow circle she'd seen Lani perform, keeping her arms as graceful as possible as she sifted through her meager range of motions. But her lack of moves didn't seem to deter Aleki, who swung closer to her as she completed the rotation, gyrating his hips. His dark eyes fastened to hers, and her heart sped up, thrumming against her breastbone in a wild tempo that far surpassed the sedate pace of the music. Adjusting the movement of his hips until they were swaying in sync with hers, back and forth, mirrored figure eight patterns. Threads of arousal stole through Stella, reaching out towards Aleki as though the invisible bonds that kept their hips moving in time could draw him closer to the sudden pulsing space covered by the thin material of her skirt. Lust hazed her vision as his grin shifted, one side hitching higher in an unmistakably dirty smirk. Her nipples tightened, straining against the lace of her bra as he let his gaze wander down her body, each pass of his eyes stroking over her so thoroughly she could imagine the hot press of his hands on her body. Tossing his head back, Aleki let out a cry, the lean column of his throat working as he claimed the air around them with his passion.

"Chee hoo!"

The sheer exuberance of his cheer reverberated through Stella, lifting the last vestiges of her discomfort and tossing them through her like the island's trade winds, until they evaporated entirely. *She* had done this. Aleki was this happy because of *her*, dancing like this, their unborn child buried deep in her womb.

The song faded, the last few bars drifting off as Aleki lowered his chin, still beaming at her.

"A magnificent performance."

"She's going to blow them away when she gets it." Lani's voice smacked of satisfaction as she strolled back into the foyer, a frosted glass of water dripping condensation in her wake. "You, though," she waggled a finger at Aleki, as she handed the glass off to Stella, who drank gratefully. "You need to match her. Too much time in meetings with Europeans, huh? Can't move like you used to."

Aleki snorted. "I've still got it."

"You've got soft, is what you've got. There's half a dozen boys down at the night market that can swing their hips better than you now."

Aleki clutched at his chest dramatically. "You wound me."

"You'll survive. And speaking of things to survive, your father sent a message."

Aleki sobered instantly, and Stella resisted the sudden pull in her stomach to reach out a hand in comfort.

Comfort isn't part of the arrangement.

"His Majesty requires me?" Aleki's forced lightness fell heavy in the wake of the good humour that had permeated their group before mention of his father.

"He requires you both." Lani nodded to Stella, drawing her into the conversation. "He has decided to hold a ball next Friday evening. A number of dignitaries and village chiefs will be in town for the Pacific rugby tournament, and he'll extend invites to others as well."

"Unusual. The official reception following the opening of the tournament usually suffices our hosting requirements. What is the purpose of this ball?"

"Ostensibly it's simply a gesture of goodwill as he tries to secure the Samoan trade deal, but in reality the understanding *loto-a* is that it's to gauge the reaction to Stella and potentially present you with alternate marriage options."

A muscle twitched in Aleki's jaw. "I see."

Fear flooded Stella and she gripped the glass tighter. "He wants you to marry someone else? Even though he knows about the baby?"

Aleki's eyes flicked towards Lani, who was now studying the tiled floor as though it held the mysteries to the universe, then back to her.

"It's a power move, a way to show he's still in control. It doesn't matter." He reached out and patted her arm and Stella tried very hard not to act like she'd been electrocuted by lust. "Lani?" Aleki continued, his focus shifting and his assistant's head bobbed up from her search for the meaning of life through mosaic.

"Yes?"

"Let's get out in front of my father, switch the narrative. We need to organise an televised interview. One that will air before next Friday. We'll announce our engagement, which should minimise any uncomfortable *Bachelor* stylings taking place at the ball. It will also solidify Stella's position as my fiancée and protect her from the worst of the fallout."

Lani's nod was decisive, the assistant's mask that had slipped during her dance lesson with Stella firmly back in place. "I'll get on that immediately, sir. In the meantime, I'll accept the king's invitation and focus Ms Warren's studies on issues most likely to be brought up during the interview. Should I arrange a stylist?"

"Stella is twenty-eight years old. She is more than capable of dressing herself appropriately. Unless -" he looked back at Stella, "you would *like* a stylist?"

"Employing someone to try and force me into marigold and salmon and hunter greens?" Stella shuddered dramatically. "Lord, no. All that colour would cause me to break out into hives."

"Good," Aleki's smile dispelled some of the tension. "I'll leave the arrangements in your capable hands, then, Lani. Come, little star. Let's show you your kingdom."

PEACE STOLE OVER STELLA, a creeping golden glow that suffused her entire being with warmth. She sat on a low wooden bench, soaking in the rays of the sun as she watched Aleki fall to the ground, clutching a rugby ball to his chest as a gaggle of school children fell upon him. Their cheers and laughter rang in the air as he fed the ball out to a small boy at the back of the makeshift ruck, who lifted it and ran with youthful ferocity into the swarm of his peers.

Aleki hauled himself to his feet as the action moved further down the sun-baked field. He'd removed his shirt before joining in the game, but his suit pants and white undershirt were streaked with dust as he jogged towards her on the sideline. An easy grin split his handsome face and his brown eyes sparkled with joy. He threw himself on the bench next to Stella and reached for one of the bottles of water strewn at her feet, the column of his throat working as he gulped half the contents down in long swallows.

"I can't keep up with these young kids nowadays."

"You are getting on in years," she commented mildly.

Rolling his eyes at her teasing, Aleki groaned. "Between the dancing and this, my ego is taking some hits today."

"Your ego could use them." Stella chuckled lightly. She paused to watch the celebrations at the far end of the field as the skinny girl who'd run the ball over the tryline held it aloft in victory. "How often do you visit the schools on the island?"

"I try to visit at least two a month. There are almost a hundred primary schools on the island and eight high schools."

"That seems like an uneven ratio."

Aleki shrugged. "A number of our young adults leave at fifteen to work, so attendance rates in the final two years are lower than the other year levels."

"Is that for financial reasons?"

"Mostly." Aleki took another sip of water, and desire fluttered deep in Stella's stomach when his tongue teased an errant drop of water from his lower lip. "Being able to support family is a key part of our value system. For some, that means attending university or trade schools, either on the island or in New Zealand, but for others the need to provide is more immediate. I've been working in tandem with our Ministers for Education and Commerce to develop alternative pathways which will allow our young people to achieve right across the economic landscape."

"That sounds like a line from a policy document."

Aleki shrugged. "It is. But it's also true. I want our young people to believe that they can achieve anything they want globally. I was born into a position of privilege, but many of my countrymen and women never leave the Pacific. They aim to live in New Zealand or Australia if they do, for the largest part. Most other countries do not even realise we exist. I want the children of Avali to know that they matter, that their work is important in a worldwide context. The pathways will take some time to gain traction, but when they do, our people will shine everywhere they put their energies."

Pride charged his voice, and Stella felt the conviction in each of his words.

"You are amazing." She didn't try to hide her admiration. She let it all flow out, let him see how in awe she was of his passion, his efforts to do right for his country. Reaching out, she squeezed his hand, ignoring the sweat and blades of grass which stuck to her skin like threads, binding them together in this new, adult relationship.

"Avali is amazing. I just want everyone to know it."

"They will." She hesitated, the words dancing on the tip of her tongue. *Just say it. The worst he can do is decline.* "I would like to help. If I can. One day.Once we've worked out what's happening with my company and I'm settled here more."

Delight lit Aleki's face and he linked his fingers through hers. "When we marry you'll be able to select a portfolio of work to address in your official capacity. Unofficially, as spokesperson for the initiative, we would be lucky to have you."

Relief bloomed in Stella, settling in her chest at his easy acceptance of her offer. Even all these years after her father leaving, and cushioned in the shadow of her mother's support, the taut pull of anxiety still stretched at her skin when she put herself forward knowing she could be rejected. It didn't matter at work, part of her job was to offer solutions and alternatives, but clients came to her for her expertise. Making unprompted offers still left her dangling in the air under the echo of Graham Warren's mocking laugh whenever she'd tried to please him. *What do you know about anything, girl? You're as useless as tits on a bull.*

"Good." Her response was soft, the usual crisp edges of her tone smoothed by Aleki's sincere acceptance of her into this part of his life.

"Hey, Prince! Are you playing or what?" The shout in English came from the pack of kids now entangled in the approximation of a scrum on the twenty-two line.

Aleki heaved a long-suffering sigh, even as the cheeky grin of his eighteen-year-old self cracked through his performance.

"Wish me luck, my princess?"

"You'll need it, Your Highness. Watch those aging knees out there."

"My knees are not nearly as injury-prone as my confidence. Will you never back me in such combat?"

Leaning forward, Stella dropped a brief kiss on his full mouth. Aleki's breath hitched and his eyes warmed. Emboldened by his reaction, she kissed him again, a sweet press of her lips to his.

"There. A token of my affection. That should be enough to win any battle."

Aleki stood to the hollering of the school children who'd witnessed their kiss and loped back onto the field his fists raised in a sign of victory. And Stella relaxed back into her tranquil cocoon, watching her future husband crash dramatically into the dirt after being tackled by an eight-year-old.

NINE

The studio lights beamed bright and hot down on Stella as a gorgeous *fa'afafine* named Velda carved cheekbones into her face with a few masterful strokes of contouring.

"That is sensational." She leaned forward, twisting her face to each side to examine it from different angles. "You're a genius."

Blunt-tipped fingers blended a spot at her jawline. "I know it, girl." The make-up artist stepped back and assessed their work. "I had a good canvas to work with though." Their compliment came out grudgingly and Stella laughed.

"I appreciate that, thank you."

"So..." Velda glanced at her from under heavily lined eyes. "You and the prince, huh?"

Stella nodded, twisting the ring on her left hand that Aleki had presented her with the night before. Nerves shot through her, little arrowheads pointing out all of her insecurities about the announcement.

You can't be what he needs! The people will resent you! He'll leave you for a nice Avalian girl!

"What I would give to be in your place." Velda fanned

themself with one hand. "I used to have a picture of him on my wall growing up, you know. My father wasn't all that accepting of my identity and he tore it down one day after I refused to sign up for rugby for another year."

Empathy rocked Stella. She wasn't the only one who knew how it felt to be uncomfortable in her role. As a *fa'afafine*, Avali's third recognised gender, Velda could surely relate to how imposter syndrome could wear on a person.

"Was it difficult for you, growing up the way you did in the islands?"

Velda shrugged, the strong muscles in their biceps bunching as they leaned forward to apply Stella's lip colour.

"It wasn't easy. I was lucky in that my mother accepted me, and that I was the youngest in my family. There are eight of us, five boys, two girls and me. So by the time I came along my father already had his sons, the whole masculine dream. But there was disappointment. It took him a long time to come to terms with who I am, and it took me a long time to come to terms with who he was, in that he couldn't accept me as myself."

Anxiety darted through Stella's blood. "Is it like that often?" The words were slightly garbled as she tried to limit the movement of her mouth. "With fathers here?"

Velda nodded, dark eyes full of resignation. "The traditional ideas still have some hold. Men want sons, they want their name to be carried forward, to be recognised as leaders in the community, the church. But it's the women who run Avali, don't you worry about that. If you need something done, you talk to a woman."

They stood back, admiring their handiwork, then nodded firmly. "Unless you need this face done. Then you talk to me."

Velda whipped the protective cape off Stella's shoulders, and she peered around them to see in the mirror. Surprise stirred in her chest. Pale rose lips and subtle highlighting gave her a blushing virgin aesthetic that anyone who had been unfortunate enough to overhear her morning vomits at Aleki's would be able to dispute. Despite nerves over the interview keeping her up all night, her green eyes looked huge and clear and her hair fell in soft Hollywood-style waves to her collarbones. Paired with her knee-length white eyelet dress and nude heels, the effect was perfect. She looked every inch the amiable bride-to-be who could have swept the prince of a small nation off his feet.

"*Manuia hine.*" The wonder in Aleki's voice was gratifying. "You look stunning."

Stella caught his eye in the mirror as he approached the makeup chair from behind. Resting a hand on her shoulder he leaned down and whispered in her ear.

"Are you ready?"

They'd gone over the questions provided by the studio last night, sprawled across her bed eating *panipopo* Lani had bought from home. She was evidently impressed by Stella's progress learning about Avali's history, politics and culture. Stella had been ecstatic upon her first experience of the soft yeasty buns baked in a sweet coconut sauce. She'd torn chunks off with her hands, dipping them in the excess syrup as she tried to craft diplomatic answers to the questions Aleki fired at her from the reef of paper.

She nodded gently, the connection of their gazes in the mirror smoothing the raw edge of apprehension that danced under her skin. She had known what he would be wearing - their outfits had been carefully selected to reflect the colours of the national flag, but she was unprepared for the sight of Aleki was dressed formally in a black lavalava and a wine-red shirt that highlighted the hint of pink in his lips. Lips that she wanted to kiss, lick, bite. The week since he'd interrupted her first dance lesson had been torture. Each afternoon Aleki came and fetched her from her lessons on history, language and culture, whirling her away to see the parts of the island known only to locals. They'd trekked a volcanic rainforest path, snorkeled coral reefs, fed the wild pigs that roamed the back roads. They'd visited The Grotto again, dining on baby octopus and taro leaves in coconut milk with Sio and his sister Oriana. And after every adventure, they'd returned back to his house so she could rest while he heated the dinners left prepared for the two of them, which they ate unfailingly on the patio as the warm island breeze brushed their skin and the South Pacific stars twinkled overhead.

She was so turned on she might die. But Aleki had remained strictly hands off since their impromptu dance. She'd turned possible reasons over and over in her head, but Velda's words spread fresh fear through her.

Is he afraid I'll have a girl? Her father had never made any secret of his disappointment at having a daughter rather than a son. A disappointment compounded by her parents' inability to have more children. Hot shame flooded her diaphragm, a familiar bite from childhood that she'd spent her adult life striving to avoid.

"I'm ready." Her words offered more assurance than she felt as she tried to push the possibility that her child might grow up feeling unwanted, burdensome by forfeit of a Y chromosome from her mind.

Her clueless fiancé smiled, and offered her his arm.

"Come little star. Let's convince the country of our love."

HEAT CRAWLED over Aleki's skin as the harsh lights burned down onto the interview stage, highlighting the artifice of the bright yellow couch, the cheery beach background. And of his deception.

Aleki shifted on the couch next to Stella, running one finger under the collar of his shirt in a futile attempt to ease the discomfort pricking at him. He was not a brave man by nature. The years he'd spent frolicking across the globe avoiding his responsibilities before Manu's accident would attest to that. But he had never wilfully tried to hoodwink his populace before. Introducing Stella as his soon-to-be-wife on national television would play into every narrative the media had ever suggested about the Playboy Prince of the Pacific's search for love. For wrong or for right, the announcement of their engagement would be seen as confirmation that he was besotted with his intended, and while it was necessary to keep Tama from running interference in his life, the idea of misleading his people sat heavy in his gut. And besides that, it had been a very long time since he gave a televised interview. His history with the press was acrimonious to say the least. Even now, with assurances given and the questions memorised, his gut screamed at him to run.

"Hey." Stella nudged him with her shoulder. "Are you okay?"

She was a vision - beauty and brains all wrapped up in one shiny, white cotton package and his apprehension faded away as he smiled at her, noting the anxious twist to her own mouth.

"A little nervous, *fafine aulelei*."

"Me too," she confessed, bending her head towards him

so they couldn't be overheard. He inhaled deeply, breathing in the crisp, clean scent of her hair as it swung forward in a lustrous curtain. "Is it because of your dad?"

"I have never defied his wishes so openly," Aleki admitted quietly. "But it needs to be done. And more than anything, your place must be cemented by my side. For the country, and also for our *pepe*."

Stella glanced at him, quickly, worriedly, a far cry from the beaming smile she usually aimed his way when he mentioned the blessing growing inside her.

"Are we all done canoodling over here?" The voice was sharp, cutting through the illusion of privacy they'd managed to create on the bustling set of Avali's premiere breakfast show. Aleki wrenched his eyes from Stella's, an unspoken question on his lips, and glanced up at the owner of the voice.

Tala Tuila was a twenty-three year old graduate of Avali University's media and communications programme. She had straight black hair, a willowy frame and a reputation as being one of the brightest stars of on-air reporting across the island. Lani's research had determined that her popularity with the under-fifties demographic would be favourable to their mixed-race marriage announcement in ways that some of the older presenters might not manage.

"Miss Tuila, it is a pleasure to meet you." He didn't stand.

"Your Highness." She didn't bow her head. "Ms Warren. We're very grateful you've given up your time this morning to appear on our show."

"We're grateful to you for having us." Stella's customer-service smile was sunny, open, and Aleki's chest tightened as he watched her practiced dazzle up at the younger woman. "Congratulations on your recent receipt of the National Fellowship in Communications."

Tala smiled slightly in return. "Thank you Ms Warren. It was an honour."

A stage assistant bustled over and caught Tala's attention, and Aleki took the opportunity to lean back over and whisper in Stella's ear.

"I don't remember seeing that in the info pack Lani provided."

Stella smirked slightly. "You didn't."

Respect for the formidable woman he was going to marry bloomed in him like the roses she loved. Before he could respond, the stage assistant pulled away from Tala and addressed them both.

"Thirty seconds, Your Highness."

As their host took a seat on the overstuffed saffron chair to their left, Aleki caught Stella's hand in his own. Squeezing quickly for reassurance, he released it just as the countdown from ten began from behind one of the large cameras.

"Talofa lava Avali, and good morning! I'm Tala Tuila and we're joined this morning by our very own Prince Aleki and a very special guest. Prince Aleki, would you care to introduce her for us?"

Aleki blinked into the lights and pasted his most charming smile on even as he mourned his corneas. Half-blinded, he recited the introduction Lani had drafted for him.

"Thank you Tala. The woman beside me is one of my oldest friends, Stella Warren. We met ten years ago at university. Stella is the owner of one of New Zealand's highest profile event management companies and a passionate supporter of various charities and human rights organisations."

"And do you and Ms Warren have any news to share with our viewers this morning?" Tala's smirk told half the story for them.

"We do." Aleki turned himself towards Stella, taking her hand as the blinking red light on the camera moved closer in his periphery. "I am thrilled to announce that I have asked Stella to be my wife, and she has agreed."

"What wonderful news!" Tala's wide smile almost met her eyes. "Congratulations to you both. Is that the ring?" She gestured to their clasped hands. "May we see?"

Stella extended her hand coyly towards Tala, ignoring the camera man who lurched frantically towards her.

"People will speculate on why I chose this ring for Stella." Aleki reclaimed Stella's hand and lifted, brushing his lips across her knuckles. His blood hummed as he caught a whiff of her crisp perfume, mixed with the coconut oil she'd used to moisturise her skin.

"I was lucky enough to be able to work with our close friend Mae Roselli to design it. The three stones represent our life together of course. Our past, at university. Our present, here together, and our future, looking forward to our life as husband and wife. It is a fitting style for a wife of a Pacific prince. Our ancestors are as much a part of our lives as our children will be." Staring directly into her eyes, Aleki took a deep breath to settle the nerves that twanged through his system like electricity, alighting with a combination of fear and honesty. Not once had Aleki Esera said these words to a woman, and whether or not she believed he was playing the part of the dutiful fiancé, the significance weighed heavily on him.

Here we go.

He rubbed his thumb gently over the largest stone in the trio, the oval lavender sapphire that sat between his grandmother's diamonds.

"This stone is for Stella." Sincerity rendered his voice husky in a way he wasn't keen to examine too closely as he addressed her directly. "Being with you reminds me of sunsets, and checklists and lavender roses. Lavender symbolises enchantment, and you have enchanted me since the first moment I met you."

This time he was sure the delicate blush that flooded her cheeks was genuine. The huge emerald pools of her eyes darted between his as the significance of the ring he'd never given voice to registered.

"How sweet. Tell me, Prince Aleki, does your family know?"

Aleki refocused on their host, frowning at the unexpected question. Lani had been crystal clear that no family questions would be acceptable in her communications with the studio. Tala leaned forward in the large presenters chair, her head tilted inquisitively to one side and the ghost of a triumphant smile hovering on her lips.

What is she playing at? Get through this and get the interview back on track. Tapping into the playboy persona he'd once worn so well, he offered her a smile of his own.

"They do now."

"How do you think they'll react?" Tala glanced at the prompt cards in her lap, though he had the distinct sense she didn't need them. Fear roiled in his belly. He knew what was coming. "Your brother in particular. After all, the last time you were infatuated with a woman he was the one to pay the price wasn't he?"

Time stood still. The thick, heavy silence pulsed in his ears, racing up his temples until it engulfed him, his skull suddenly too small for the fog of rage that enveloped his brain.

"This interview is over." His voice sounded foreign, ripped out of the hollow where his stomach had been, laid out before them like five miles of gravel road, rough and raw.

"But Your Highness -"

"Over." Aleki glared at the camera operator, holding the other man's gaze until the blinking red light went dark.

Aleki glared at Tala, letting her feel every ounce of his anger in the heat of his gaze.

"Bold choice."

Tala raised her chin slightly, defiance etched into the line of her jaw. "Fortune favours the brave."

"Does it?" He kept his voice silky even as the beast inside him thrashed. "And how much fortune might one need to cover a sustained period of unemployment?" He stood, ignoring the blanch that stole over Tala's dark skin and extended his hand to Stella, whose distress was palpable in the tight grip of her fingers around his. "Excuse us, please."

He strode off the stage into the darkness that matched his soul, dragging his intended behind him.

TEN

The warm leather barely moved under the force of Aleki's punch. He threw another, harder, as though the boxing bag would somehow have weakened its defenses in the last half hour of constant attack. A flurry followed, thick and fast, combinations from his childhood lessons that were as much a part of his DNA as his hair or eyes. The bag swayed gently, mocking him, as though his fists were of no more consequence than an island breeze. He caught it mid-bob, leaning his forehead against the smooth surface, his breath sawing out of him in ragged exhalations only partially related to exercise.

"Is this a private party, or can anyone join?"

Even through emotional and physical exhaustion, Stella's voice burrowed inside him, a soft candlelight glow. It smoothed the rusty edges of his fear, stroking back and forth until the tension that bunched his shoulders loosened its violent grip.

"I don't think this is the kind of party you're used to, *fafine aulelei.*"

"Ridiculous," she scoffed gently, her voice gaining

strength as she moved closer. "Any party is my kind of party. If I'd known this was coming I would have set up refreshments in the corner." A light touch drifted down his naked back, settling at the base of his spine. "Are you okay?"

Exhaling heavily, he shook his head. His fingers tightened on the bag as though it could protect him from the questions that were coming.

"Okay. Do what you have to do. I'll be over here if you need me."

That's it?

He raised his head from the bag, watching as she settled on a mat at the far side of his weights room. She leaned back against the mirrored wall, crossing her legs and pulling a book out of the bag slung across her chest. Gone was the sweet sundress she'd worn to the interview, swapped for a silky white top with delicate shoulder straps and a swishy black skirt.

"You don't want to know what she was talking about?" He forced the words out past the knot of fear in his throat. He'd never voluntarily spoken to anyone about Manu's accident. Never.

Stella placed the book in her lap and looked up. Across the room he could almost believe she didn't feel the tendrils of desperation reaching out from him, begging her to say no, to tell him he never had to think about it again.

"Yes," she said simply. "I want to know, because it hurt you. It's *still* hurting you, and I'm not okay with that. But I'm not going to pry, Aleki. Whatever it is, it's clearly not something you want to delve into. If you're ready to tell me one day, you will. For now, I'm just going to sit here and read so you're not alone while it eats you up."

With each word, the golden light in his chest expanded a little further, pushing back the black abyss of dread until it shrank back down to its regular mango-sized lump under his ribs.

She deserves to know, the voice in his head declared with some authority. *It will affect her too, in the long run.*

Fuck off, the eminantly more sensible part of his brain responded. Still, the kernel was there and he rolled it over in his brain, looking at it from different angles, trying to ignore the screaming warning that she'd leave him if she knew.

Gritting his teeth, he stared at her while he unwrapped his knuckles. She flicked a page in her book, then a second, likely aware of his scrutiny but ignoring it.

"Okay." His voice sounded like five miles of gravel road, but Stella lit up at his surly acceptance. "Let's go."

He pulled on a black tee and headed towards the door. The slap of her flat sandals followed and he knew without looking that she was grinning all the way down the hallway and out the back door as he headed towards the garage.

He caught a glimpse of that sunshine smile as she swung into the truck cab next to him and he gunned the ignition. The nondescript black pickup blended in on the island roads and had the four wheel drive he needed.

Stella stayed silent as they wove their way inland, the truck creeping higher in the hills with every mile. Finally, Aleki pulled off the road and hopped out to open an ordinary looking farm gate on the side of the road. He drove the vehicle through, then threw the parking brake on as he got out to shut the gate again. When he returned to the cab, she was eyeing him suspiciously.

"Is this where I need to lie about my martial arts training again?"

Aleki huffed a small laugh through the tightness in his throat.

"Not at all." Putting the truck in gear, he rolled slowly

forward, following the beaten farm track as it lazed down into a hidden valley.

"You know how I am about my privacy at the house?"

"I do." She would have signed waiver upon waiver before arriving in Avali for Mae and Luke's wedding, and nobody could miss the security measures at the front gate, or the patrols by the cliffside beach access point.

"Well, the house is my oasis. I built to get away from the responsibilities of royal life that haunt me in the city. It's my place of peace, my paradise."

"Sure."

The truck bumped down the bottom of the hill, cruising to a stop on the flat expanse of land that stretched before them. A small lake glittered amongst the native green bush, a rickety wooden platform extending out over the water's edge. Just being here, Aleki felt the roil of fear and loathing in his stomach recede.

"The house is my oasis," Aleki repeated. "But this is my hiding place." He gestured to the left, and Stella peered past the steering wheel. He could tell when she saw the small wooden structure camouflaged in the trees. Her head tilted to the side, her fresh scent wafting up from her hair and helping ease the last of his doubt.

"And why does the prince of a tropical island need a hiding place?"

A grimace twisted his mouth.

"Come, *fafine aulelei*. I'll tell you inside."

'Inside' was something of a misnomer. The *fale* was built in traditional island style. A rectangular slab of concrete made up the foundation, while rough-hewn logs marched along the edges, supporting the sheets of corrugated iron that made up the roof. There were no walls, and the only furniture within the structure was a low, overstuffed sofa, a small dining table with two chairs and a wooden bedframe and mattress made up with a simple navy quilt. A small refrigerator with an electric kettle on top hummed quietly in one corner and a single light bulb swung gently from the ceiling.

Aleki lowered himself onto the sofa, his body folding into the familiar curves and dips of the broken springs. Stella sat at the other end, her sandalled feet tucked under her as she surveyed the dwelling.

"I built this place four years ago." His voice pulled her attention to him, and he felt the caress of her green eyes over his face as surely as if she'd reached out and touched him.

"I lived here for six months. Nobody except Lani and Andreas knew where I was. They delivered the generator, the construction materials and the furniture. Andreas bought food out weekly, Lani made sure I had books to read, but for the most part I was completely alone. I fished in the lake, ate the coconuts and bananas that grow around the property, cooked every now and then in the fire pit out the back. Nobody else has ever been here."

"Why are you showing me this place?" Stella's question was careful, as if she understood how much of himself he was revealing with this trip.

Sucking the air into his lungs, he continued. "A few months before I came here, I was dating a woman. Beautiful, accomplished, a nice island family. The king was pleased, and I was twenty-four and happy to please him. She and I didn't have a lot in common, but we enjoyed each other's company. At one point we took a trip to London together, chaperoned by her brother of course. But that's where the trouble started."

He fiddled with a loose thread at the hem of his sports

shorts. Bright red, it drew the eye like a thin streak of blood against the dark hair of his thigh. The air swelled around him as he focused on running the thread between his fingers, eyes down to avoid Stella's gaze, which weighed on him as heavily as the memories he sifted through to help her understand.

"We went out one night. Nothing special, a bar, a club. The playboy-prince narrative hadn't caught hold yet but there were enough foreign press around that we were noticed. She didn't seem to mind, and I didn't care either way. She popped off to the bathroom at one stage and her brother and I joked around until she returned. When she got back, she wanted to leave, so we did."

The images flickered through his brain, bright pulses of light thrumming through the cracks of the box in his mind where he'd relegated all thoughts of that particular night.

"Where did you go?" Stella's quiet question drew him back to the present.

"We went back to the hotel." He huffed out a sigh. "I went to my room, and she and her brother went to theirs. It's not the done thing in Pacific cultures to sleep together before marriage, and although we'd had sex before, we pretended we hadn't to keep her reputation intact. But that night, she came to me and one thing led to another." Aleki twisted the thread so tightly around the top of his finger that purple shadowed the skin around his nail.

"It wasn't the same as usual though. She told me to do things - to *say* things - that we hadn't tried before. And I was young and full of hormones, far away from Avali, so I did."

The sourness of regret lingered at the back of his throat and he swallowed heavily, hoping it would wash away the bitter taste.

"She sold the story the next morning to a tabloid. She'd

arranged it in the bathroom at the club. There was an audio recording... Nothing bad by Western standards, but the evidence of us having sex, coupled with some of my language and my position made waves." He drifted off, snippets of soundbites ringing in his ears mockingly.

"Jesus, what a bitch." Stella's breathy murmur was tinged with incredulity.

Aleki shook his head quickly. "No. No, she wasn't. She left a note. It turned out her nice island family was nothing of the sort. She was the victim of domestic abuse. Her letter explained that she meant to use the money to escape, to start a new life away from her parents and her brother. She was a young, scared woman, raised in horrible circumstances and when she saw the opportunity to escape, she did so. I cannot hold that against her, even if she sacrificed me on the altar of public opinion to do so."

"I see." Stella's tone revealed nothing and he snuck a glance at her, serious green eyes surveying him over ruffle-covered knees.

"The family was investigated, of course. She had a younger sister who was sent to live with an aunt. Her father lost his job over the charges and they've been shunned for the most part."

"Yet you're the one who lived in the bush?"

A sigh rumbled up through his chest. "It's complicated. I've spoken to you before about shame, about how it affects us here. This scandal was unprecedented by an Avalian royal in modern times. My father lost it - screaming, throwing things, cursing me to the ancient gods. I escaped here - this land belonged to my mother's family and it passed to me upon her death. Manu has his own section north on the island. I'd never actually spent any time here before, but I was scared. Scared to face my father, my people. Scared of the shame I had brought upon myself and my country in the eyes of the international press. Reporters were swarming the island. Every time Lani delivered food she mentioned the number of them, the breaches of security at the house, the interview requests. It was the first time I'd felt that level of scrutiny, and it had nothing to do with my work or my status, merely how I like to fuck. So I ran, and I hid."

"Just like she did."

A tight smile twisted his lips. "Yes, *fafine aulelei*. Just like she did."

"And did they find you?"

"No." He lifted his head and caught her gaze. "They found Manu."

Her brow crumpled and he hurried to explain. "Since Manu was nine, he's wanted to play rugby league professionally. He trained every day, he watches game tapes to relax. It's his passion. He finally made it at a club in Sydney five years ago. He was home during the Australian off-season when there was a car accident. A pack of reporters, looking for information on me outside his gym in Havalei'i. One journo got too close following him home, clipped the rear of his car. Manu's car smashed into a fence. His best friend Tua died, and Manu broke his leg in three places. The damage was extraordinary. Doctors weren't sure he'd ever be able to play again. It took him two and a half years of surgeries and rehab before he stepped on a footy field after that. The shame I felt from the tape was nothing compared to knowing that my cowardice cost our friend his life and almost cost my brother his dream."

"Oh, Aleki." Stella's hand reached out, gently untangling the wound thread from where it bit into the skin of his finger, and smoothing over the back of his hand gently. "You can't blame yourself for that. Accidents happen."

"No." He shook his head empathetically. "If I'd stood my ground, if I hadn't let fear drive me from my responsibilities, they would never have been at risk. Manu would never have been injured." He looked up, catching her gaze and holding it. "He has forgiven me, but I cannot forgive myself. That is why I can never have a real relationship. That's why you've signed non-disclosure agreements, and why I had Luke draft a contract. This marriage will be my only one, little star, but I will not let emotions make a fool of me again. I will honour you, protect you, raise our child with you, but I can never love you. Love makes men weak, and I am too scared of my own weakness to knowingly enter into that position again." He reached up and tucked a swath of silky hair behind her ear. "This will have to be enough."

STELLA KNEADED the bread mixture harder than was probably necessary, pulling and folding and working her frustration into the dough.

"Girl." Lani was not amused. "*Panipopo* need to be made with love. You're going to serve those up to His Highness and crack one of his teeth."

"Good." Stella used her forearm to push her hair out of her face so she could focus on the other woman, who sat cool and serene at the breakfast bar while Stella sweated over her recipe for Aleki's favourite treat. "He deserves it. Did you know he blames himself for his brother's accident?"

Lani carefully lowered the tablet she was tapping on to the marble benchtop before meeting Stella's eyes.

"He talked to you about Manu and Tua?"

She huffed in response, thwacking the dough again.

"Stella, listen to me." Lani's seriousness cut through the yeast-scented heat of the kitchen. "He never talks about what happened to Manu and Tua. *Never.*"

"Well, it was a long time ago, I suppose."

"No. Never. Not to Manu himself. Not to me. Not to the king, or Sio, or the four different therapists I organised for him to meet with when he stumbled out of the bush looking like a skinny yeti. When the accident happened I went to see him immediately. He thanked me for the information and told me to go home. The next day he was back here, shaving and working and dressing the part of the playboy prince they started calling him. But he never spoke of it."

Unease trickled down Stella's spine, chilling her despite the muggy heat of the kitchen.

"But why would he tell me?" Aleki had made it clear that their relationship was one of circumstance, not care. It didn't make sense that he'd share something so private with her if he meant to keep her at arm's length.

Lani raised one perfectly shaped brow, and brushed an imaginary speck of lint off the shoulder of her yellow *pule-tasi* dress.

"Perhaps there is a reason His Highness was so quick to rip up the contract for your marriage."

Stella scoffed, wrestling down the familiar sting of hope that snapped in her chest at Lani's suggestion.

"I'm afraid His Highness has been quite clear about his expectations for his marriage." She pummelled the dough once more, then tossed it in the lightly oiled bowl to rise. "We are mutually beneficial to each other. No doubt my usefulness merely extends to acting as a subpar counsellor. After all, I've already signed an NDA." Stella moved quickly to cover the bread bowl, her teeth worrying the inside of her cheek.

"Maybe." Lani picked up the tablet again and scrolled through something, as she continued mildly. "But maybe not."

A shrill ring cut through the air. Stella rolled her eyes at Lani's romanticism even as she dug in her apron pocket for her cellphone, swiping to accept the call without even looking at the screen.

"Stella Warren speaking."

"Hey there, girlie."

Her stomach dropped as the grizzled voice sawed through the speaker.

"How did you get this number?"

"What kind of greeting is that for your dear old Dad?"

Stella puffed a humourless laugh. "Hello, Graham. How lovely to hear from you. Tell me, do you need picking up from the cells, or money to cover your gambling debts? Either way, I'm unable to help."

"Yeah, yeah, saw you were out of the country. There's a bit on the news sites about you. Something about marrying a prince from one of those islands."

Stella said nothing, letting the silence stretch across the phone and oceans.

"Anyways, girlie, just wanted to check on you. See how you're getting on."

"I'm well, thank you."

"Good to hear, good to hear." A rasping cough, tinged with age and emphysema rattled down the line. "Looks like you're doing pretty well for yourself."

"I've been doing well for myself for years. Since before Mum died. We missed you at the funeral."

"Ah, you know me, girlie. Not really one for the show-manship. Mary and I had already said our goodbyes."

"Have you already said goodbye to her life insurance payout? Is that why you're calling?

A grim chuckle. "You were always hard on me, girlie. But look where I got you. Fancy career, nice place in the city, a rich husband."

"You told me I wasn't worth the time it would take to teach me how to ride a bike."

"Ah, well, I could be a bit tough sometimes. I always wanted a boy, you know."

Hot tears pricked behind Stella's lashes as she fought to keep her voice steady. "Yeah, Dad. You've mentioned that before. Anyway, I have to go now. Great chat." She stabbed at the red button with a shaking finger as Aleki rushed into the kitchen with Lani on his heels.

"Stella?" Strong arms wrapped around her, squeezing tight while she heaved in a gasping breath.

In and out. In and out. In and out.

"Are you okay? Lani said your dad called."

"Mmm. Mmm hmmm." Stella nodded, concentrating on taking, slow exhales and doing her best not to nuzzle her soon-to-be husband. There was only so much she could take in one day from men who were supposed to love her.

The thought stopped her cold, breath and all. Her complicated feelings for her father were one thing - one thing she paid an exorbitant amount of money to discuss with a professional - but the idea that Aleki was supposed to love her rolled around in her head, foreign and uncomfortable.

Moments strung together in an internal slideshow - clips of an eighteen-year-old Aleki smiling at her in their local pub, bringing her chop suey for their study sessions, an adult Aleki determined on her doorstep after discovering the pregnancy, pressing his palm against her still-flat belly before drifting off to sleep, confessing his darkest shame to her on a broken-down couch. For a woman who prided herself on her attention to detail, she hadn't even noticed she'd gone and fallen in love with the man who was marrying her out of obligation.

The realisation struck her swift and furiously.

Holy shit, I love him. Of all the stupid, irrational things to do.

"Shhh," Aleki shushed her, stroking up and down her back in slow, soothing movements. "It's okay. It will all be okay."

Humiliation thrummed through her blood, thick and hot. How pathetic, to pine for someone who saw you as merely a means to an end. Stella straightened her spine, pushing back from Aleki's warm embrace. He dropped his arms slowly, those deep chocolate eyes still searching her face with concern.

"Yes." She pasted on a smile and met his gaze steadily. "It will all be okay. I just had a wobbly moment, that's all. But I'm old enough and smart enough to know when to give up." Her laugh was brittle. "Is there anything worse in the world than a girl who just sits around waiting to be loved?"

Aleki eyed her warily. "It's okay to feel hurt," he offered, gently. "When someone hurts you."

"No." A firm shake of her head. "I should know better. Love is my business. All I need is to know that this child, our pepe -" she held her hand over her stomach "-will always feel loved. Nothing else matters." She reached out and cupped his cheek, the warm skin of his cheek flooding her palm.

"Thank you for the reminder."

ELEVEN

Aleki paced up and down the foyer, fiddling with his wooden cufflink. Cut from the branches of a local hibiscus tree, the links had been crafted by a master carver to represent the crest of Avali. His cousins Sio and Oliana had gifted them to him for his twenty-first birthday and they were one of his most prized possessions. Wearing them tonight to attend his father's ball with Stella at his side felt right. Spending time with her, preparing for the baby had finally made him feel ready. If the mantle of sovereignty was placed upon his shoulders, he could cope. More than that, he could thrive. A rush of certainty raced through him. He could conquer anything as long as Stella was by his side. Never had he dared to hope that a shotgun marriage of convenience might so profitable to his own goals.

"You look incredible." Her voice startled him, coming from the balustrade. Gazing up, he snagged her eyes, before letting his eyes travel down the length of her body. Everything stopped for a single moment. But one moment was enough. When time started again, along with his heart and his ability to breathe, he was dizzy with transformation.

O la'u ia. She is mine.

"You are wearing colour." The words rasped through the dryness in his throat, gravel peppering the air.

Stella beamed as she descended the stairs. "The colour of our national flag. Don't get used to it, but I'm thinking it might be patriotic to pop a few red pieces into rotation."

"Let me have a proper look."

She stood back proudly, almost eye level with him in her heels. Scarlet silk fell in waves to the floor and encased her to the wrist. The pleated bodice hugged her torso to her throat, skimming across her curves in a way that made him palms itch, save for the slivers of creamy skin that peeked out from subtle diagonal slits along her collarbones.

"Exquisite."

Stella's smile widened, joy radiating off her. "Do you really like it?"

"I have never seen a more stunning woman in all of my life." Sincerity pooled in his words, weighing them with the force of his desire.

"You don't think I should have put my hair up?"

"No." He caught an errant caramel strand, and rubbed it between his fingers. "No fancy hairstyle. No heavy-handed makeup. You are enough. And you, in this dress? *Fafine aulelei*, you could have the world."

The sound of her delight bounced off the tile of his entrance way, as she tugged him towards the door.

"And who would give me the world, Aleki?"

I would.

As soon as the car began moving down the driveway, he hit the button for the privacy window and slid across the backseat. The crisp scent of her teased at his nostrils as he nuzzled against the satin skin of her neck.

"Want to make out?"

"Oh, the romance of it all," Stella quipped. She surveyed him again. "How would I even get into your pants? If that were my intention," she added at his raised eyebrow.

A chuckle bubbled out of Aleki. Truthfully, the formal sarong-like *lavalava* came to almost his ankles, and the bulkiness of the woven pandanas cloth over it would make any downstairs action almost impossible for him. But for her?

"Your intentions have been duly noted. But for now, perhaps we could focus on me getting into yours?"

"Perhaps we could." A smirk played over her full lips. "If I were wearing any."

Blood rocketed to his groin.

"*Tagaloa.*" The name of the deity slipped out on an exhalation, the mere thought of his finacee bare beneath her dress enough to offer up a prayer of thanks or a plea for strength, he knew not which.

Sliding to his knees on the thick pile of the car's interior, he ran his hands up the smooth muscles of her calves.

"Aleki!" Stella's whisper was laced with alarm. "What are you doing? Get up!"

"I am up, *fafine aulelei*. I could not be higher or harder. You will pay for that." He placed a kiss on the inside of her knee as he pushed the skirts of her dress higher.

"We are in a *car!*" She sounded scandalised. It was adorable.

Even as his hands bunched the folds of her dress at her hips, he looked up and caught her eyes. Apprehension warred with excitement in their emerald depths. Holding Stella's gaze, Aleki spoke slowly but firmly.

"If you think there is one place on this island or God's green earth that I will not take you as my own, you are mistaken. You are precious to me, and I welcome any opportunity to worship you on my knees."

Stella's face softened. Cupping his cheek in her hand, she leaned forward and dropped a sweet kiss on his lips.

"My Prince Charming."

Aleki skated his eyes down as she settled back against the plush leather. He held her legs open and marvelled at the sight of his hands against the honeyed flesh of her thighs. The contrast of her light tan with his darker skin was like a sepia-toned picture; shades of their desire painted across the surface of their bodies.

He bent his head to her hip, trailing soft open-mouthed kisses along the satin of her skin.

"Aleki!"

"Shhh, little star." He nuzzled the top of her thigh. "It is rude for me to speak with my mouth full."

Propping his fingers under the lush curve of her behind, he put his lips on her. Spurred on by Stella's quick intake of breath, he ran his tongue lazily down the centre of her, lapping at her entrance. The return journey took longer. He dragged his tongue over each centimeter of her succulent flesh and then back again, climbing higher each time until he finally swiped across the bundle of nerves at the top.

Pleasure laced with pain coursed through him as Stella gripped his hair and hissed her approval.

Humming in satisfaction, he closed his lips around the tiny bud. Suckling softly, he teased at her entrance with a finger, easing in as he laved his tongue across her sweet spot. The heat of Stella clenching against his fingers ratcheted Aleki's own arousal and he growled his desire against her delicate flesh. The pressure increased as he added a second digit. He looked up sharply to see rapture etched on her face in stark relief, a vision in red as her back arched against the seat.

"Look at me, Stella."

She wrenched her eyes to his and he felt it as soon as their gazes crashed onto one another. The pulse of her passion deep inside. His tongue slid out once more and pressed against her intimately, nothing but heat and pressure on her most sensitive spot. Green fire flashed in her eyes as she watched him watching her. Then she was cresting, the tight wet pull of her swallowing his fingers as her thighs shook under the grip of his other hand and she cried out, a hushed keen that would ring in his memory for eternity.

She sank back against the seat, one hand languidly reaching out to caress his shoulder as she hummed her satisfaction.

He had just finished rearranging her dress, smoothing the fabric over her thighs when the car pulled to a stop.

"Do I look alright?" Nerves stilted Stella's voice as she fluffed her hair. Aleki returned the traditionally patterned fabric square he'd been using to discreetly wipe his mouth to the pocket of his collarless black dress shirt and caught one of her hands as it threaded through her silken waves.

"You look even more beautiful now than you did half an hour ago."

"Charmer." Linking her fingers with his, she squeezed. "You'll take care of me in there?"

"Nothing could stop me."

"Let's do it then."

He rushed around the back of the car to beat Andreas there, to be the one to open her door and reveal her to the waiting media. Pride swelled in him at the collective intake of breath and the flashes of cameras that met her as she stepped out of the car. She was so poised that anyone unaware of the situation might have suspected she'd been born to this life. He offered her his arm and ate up the secret smile she bestowed upon him as she took it.

The Avali media and few international reporters stationed at the entrance to the palace were respectful and polite. Tala was conspicuously absent. Aleki answered several questions on his way in and he and Stella both accepted congratulations on their engagement. Just before they crossed the threshold, Aleki paused and passed a small envelope to a member of King Tama's staff.

"What was that?" Stella enquired as they meandered down the main hallway, lined with paintings of former rulers.

Aleki shrugged. "A token of goodwill for the local reporters."

"You paid them?" She sounded incredulous.

"I offered them a small gift for their kindness towards us. The international media is a slavering beast, it will eat a person up and spit out the bones without remorse. This is not the Pacific way, but globalisation can be either a friend or a foe. The local media have given up time with their families to be here tonight outside of their work hours. Nobody shouted obnoxious questions at us and they didn't take pictures of you until you were completely out of the car, with your dress in place. That is the spirit of Polynesia, and it deserves to be rewarded."

"But journalism is supposed to be free from politics."

A deep belly laugh rumbled up out of him. "Oh, little star, my token will not exclude me from criticism. The papers will tell me exactly what they think of my choices, both political and personal. But they will not be unnecessarily rude. They will not buy tawdry photographs from other countries when we take our honeymoon. And most of the gift will go back into the local economy. For some families, it may mean a school trip for their oldest, a pair of rugby boots or a new book, a special night out for the parents where they can reconnect with each other. When you give with good intentions, that goodness lives on in the recipient."

"What a gorgeous sentiment." Stella's approval wrapped around Aleki like a blanket. She continued, with a smirk. "So, tawdry photographs huh?"

"Do you doubt it?"

"Never." Her grin lit up the hallway. "And where might this honeymoon take place?"

Before Aleki could answer, the clearing of a throat behind him caught their attention. Twisting his head, he spotted the familiar face of Iosefa, his father's personal secretary.

"Your Highness."

"Iosefa."

The older gentleman nodded towards Stella. "Miss."

"Fa'alofa." She greeted Iosefa in flawless Avalian, dipping her head in acknowledgement.

"His Majesty would like to speak with you privately, Your Highness."

"Now?"

"Yes, Your Highness. It is a matter of some import."

Aleki fought the urge to roll his eyes. King Tama had always been somewhat prone to dramatics, but this was out of hand.

"Where?"

Iosefa gestured to a wooden door off to the side of the hallway. A heavy sigh wrenched from Aleki's lips as he turned back towards Stella.

"I'll be right back, little star. Amuse yourself by reading about how my ancestors fought off yours in the plaques beside the paintings."

"Such fun." She patted his bicep lightly. "Go be a prince. I'll stand here in my princess dress and do my history homework."

Aleki strode towards the door, frustration pulling at his chest. Throwing the door open he entered the small room, only to gasp in surprise.

"Manu!"

"Aleki!" His brother moved towards him and swept him up in a hug. At six feet two, they were evenly matched in height, but Manu's heavily muscled frame was wider and his arms felt like iron bars across Aleki's back.

Standing back, Aleki surveyed his brother quickly. The riot of curls that usually fell below Manu's shoulders were slicked back, styled into two smooth braids. Like Aleki, he wore a tapa and formal shirt in grey. Light wrinkles were etched around his eyes, evidence of his zest for life. However, Aleki noted darker shadows under his eyes. Altogether, his younger brother looked wearier than he had the last time he'd seen him at Christmas.

"You're doing well?"

"I'm doing better than you." Manu slapped his arm. "You're getting married? To some *palagi* girl?"

Aleki grinned. "You'll love her. She's incredible."

"She clearly has no taste if she's marrying you."

"That's enough." Tama's voice cut through their lighthearted ribbing, heavy with authority. Switching to their native language, he continued. "You are here for a reason, both of you. Please be seated."

Exchanging looks, they sat facing Tama behind the room's desk.

The king steepled his fingers in front of his chest. "Aleki, I trust from the interview you gave that you are insistent on moving forward with this foolish plan."

"It is not a foolish plan, Father. Stella is thoughtful, intelligent and she will be an excellent mother. She is precisely the kind of woman I need by my side as I prepare for leadership."

Tama scoffed, huffing his scorn into the air like a weapon. "And what leadership would that be, boy? You think I will turn my country over to a pair of children to squabble over as they try to make an impossible relationship work?"

"It is not impossible."

"It is!" The king's eyes flashed with anger. "She knows nothing of our people, our way of life. She will go back to her world and you will be the laughingstock of Polynesia. We are too close to closing the trade deal with Samoa to allow for your childish behaviour to detract from our goal."

"What do you propose as a solution then, Father? Abandoning my child so I can serve?"

"No. That would bring shame upon us that Avali cannot shoulder. You will have to marry her and you will have to stay with her. That is the example our people expect us to set. But you cannot rule with her alongside you. Manu will take your place."

"What?" Manu's voice matched the horror swelling in Aleki at his father's threat.

"I am the heir." Aleki leapt to his feet, anger pulsing through his veins in a sticky beat. "My whole life has been in preparation for this. You cannot punish me for choosing a partner you do not agree with."

"I most certainly can." King Tama's beady eyes

narrowed in satisfaction. "I will announce it following your wedding."

Aleki's mind whirred as the implications slotted into place, looking for an escape. *He can't take this from me. It is my destiny to serve the people. Everything I have done has been for them. The climate change agreement, the tourism budget, the Samoa deal.*

"The Samoa deal!" He blurted it out before he could even finish the thought.

Tama fixed him with a glare. "What about it?"

"If I can close the deal, if I can establish a long-term working trade agreement with Samoa to provide resources to the European Union as we have been aiming for for the last eighteen months, will that prove to you that I am mature enough to rule once you step down?"

His father stroked his mustache slowly. "It might."

"With Stella as my wife. That is not negotiable."

After what seemed like an age, the king nodded. "You have one month. If the Samoa deal is secured and signed one month from today I will agree to bless the marriage of you and the woman. But this is it, Aleki. No more chances. If you fail to secure the deal, Manu becomes my heir."

Aleki reached out and clasped his father's paw in his own. The anger that had bled through him morphed into adrenaline. He could do this. One month of hard work and his role would be secure. In the monarchy and in his marriage. One month from now and he would have it all.

TWELVE

The door opened behind Stella and she was nearly knocked off her feet by the wave of tension that billowed out in her fiancé's wake.

Face tight, dark eyes shuttered, he stalked towards her purposefully.

"Let's go."

"Woah," she placed a hand on his forearm, squeezing gently. "Are you okay? Would you like some water?"

Dark eyes flicked between her own and her hand.

"I just need to get inside. There are important people to meet with."

Unease slithered up her spine. As Aleki grasped her hand and tugged, she caught sight of two other men exiting the room he'd come from. King Tama, regal in his traditional clothing, and beautiful younger man who looked like a cross between a professional wrestler and Heidi, with two long, thick plaits of hair hanging over his shoulders. Tama stared through her, but the other man ran his eyes over her in blatant appraisal.

"Who's that?" She scurried after Aleki as he marched towards the double doors to The Great Hall.

"My brother." His answer was curt.

"Your brother is here? Should I say hello?"

"You'll meet him soon, I'm certain. He'll make sure of it."

As they approached the doors and the sound of drums became louder, Stella stopped walking and pulled their clasped hands towards her body. Aleki turned, looking directly at her for the first time since he'd exited the small room.

"Aleki?"

"Stella?"

"Are you sure you're alright?" Butterflies thumped against the walls of her stomach as though they were trying to escape.

Aleki smiled quickly, a tight movement across the slash of this mouth that did nothing to alleviate her fears.

"I will be, little star. Tonight is an important night for both of us. It is essential to present ourselves well. We cannot show any weakness if we wish to be taken seriously as a couple. The stakes are high, but I have faith in you."

"And us?"

Another smile that didn't meet his eyes.

"Of course, *fafine aulelei*. In us."

Reluctantly, Stella allowed herself to be led towards the doors. Lani had explained earlier in the week that only King Tama would be announced formally, so she was unsurprised to walk in without fanfare. What did surprise her was the reception. Hot prickles of awareness crawled over her skin as she felt the eyes of the room zero in on her.

You should have known this would happen. He's one of

the most eligible men in the world and he decided to marry you out of nowhere.

The thought did little to alleviate the uncomfortable sensation of being watched, but she was grateful that she'd taken time while Aleki was in his meeting to touch up her makeup after the events of the limo ride.

"Matai ali'i!" Aleki's enthusiastic greeting to an older gentleman pulled her attention back to her circumstances. He bowed low in front of the other man and extended his hand. As per Lani's instructions, Stella also bowed and shook the hands of him and his female companion as Aleki made introductions.

"Stella, this is High Chief Alo of Samoa and his wife Seini. Matai, this is my fiancée, Stella Warren."

"Talofa lava," Stella murmured, trying frantically to remember any Samoan past the basic greeting. There were similarities between Avalian and Samoan but her mind was blank as she grasped for them.

"It is a pleasure to meet you," High Chief Alo spoke in flawless English. "Congratulations on your upcoming nuptials."

Stella's short-lived relief soon faded when it became clear that she was not going to be called on for any further discourse. Instead, Aleki and Alo became engrossed in a supernaturally tedious conference about export. After an initial struggle to understand their conversation, Stella gave up in favour of smiling at Seini like a simpleton and staring around the room.

And so it went. Introduction after introduction to stodgy old men, often with wives, sometimes with adult children; then a thousand dull discussions she had no hope of understanding. The sole bright spot was a brief moment with Sio and his sister Oliana, a sweet girl in her early twenties, before Aleki was whirling her across the hall with a determined set of his jaw to engage yet another diplomat in dreary conversation.

Eventually tiring of pasting her most dazzling smile on while compiling multiple to-do lists in her head, she leapt in during a brief respite in conversation.

"Excuse me, gentlemen. I'll be right back."

Elation pounded in her veins as she picked her way through the Great Hall and towards the corridor where the bathrooms were located. *Freedom!*

Once inside a stall, she flipped the lid down and sat on top of it. Dropping her head towards her knees, she inhaled deeply, pulling in oxygen and letting it revive her brain cells after what seemed like an eternity spent in smiling, nodding hell.

"Did you see the woman?" Scorn dripped from its owner's voice as the door swung open, ushering in a clatter of heels and waft of perfume. Any semblance of calm Stella had claimed shattered, retreating in the presence of such commotion.

"What on earth is Aleki thinking?" Bitterness tinged the speaker's tone. "She has nothing to offer. No family, no connections, and she's as plain as day to look at."

Horror bloomed in Stella's stomach as she realised they were talking about her.

"That's not kind, Sabrina," an accented voice chided gently. "She could be a nice person. We haven't spoken to her yet."

"And we're not going to speak to her, either," Sabrina the Bitter claimed, over the sound of the tap splashing against porcelain. "She looks like a veritable prostitute."

Oh, hell no.

The door was open before she could stop herself. "What are you talking about? This is a *full-length* gown. It has *long sleeves* and a *jewel neckline.*"

The two women standing at the counter gaped at her. Both had black hair teased into intricate updos, and wore brightly patterned dresses with woven flax overskirts. Recognition dawned on Stella as they gawped at her and she drew herself up to her full height, nodding once at the shorter of the two.

"Your Highness."

The Crown Princess of Tonga recovered first. "Ms Warren, I must ask you to excuse Sabrina's outburst. My cousin from Nuie has a lot to learn about diplomacy." Despite her petite stature, she fixed her companion with an intimidating glare. "Please be assured it will not happen again. We wish you and Prince Aleki every happiness."

"Thank you for your good wishes. It would be an honour to speak to you regarding your work around literacy in the Pacific, but I fear now is not the right time. Please excuse me, ladies."

She swept past the pair, focused entirely on exiting the room with some semblance of grace. Surprise registered a moment later as she glided into the hallway only to bump into a solid wall of masculinity.

Aleki's brother reached out to steady her, his fingers warm through the fabric of her sleeve.

"Careful there, *palagi.*"

Irritation surged through Stella, robbing her of her sense of propriety. This was ridiculous. She was being bounced around from one crappy situation to the next without a chance to catch her breath.

"Can I help you?" Her words were hot with exasperation. "Or were you merely lying in wait to grab at any woman leaving the bathroom?"

Her assailant startled her by throwing his head back and laughing. A throaty rumble echoed down the corridor, and Stella tried very hard not to punch a prince.

"Oh, I see now. This is going to be fun." Hooking her hand through his arm, Aleki's brother started them back towards the hall. "I was looking for you actually."

"In the toilets? How very George Michael of you. And what did you want with me?"

Another dynamite grin. Even through the fog of her frustration, Stella could acknowledge that these Esera men were hell on the hormones.

"I wanted to introduce myself. I didn't get the chance earlier. My name is Manu Esera, and I understand that you are going to be my new sister-in-law."

Suspicion coloured her response. "It's nice to meet you, Manu. My name is Stella Warren, and I understand that you have upset my fiancé in some way."

A slab of muscle lifted and fell as Manu shrugged casually. "Nothing to do with me, Ms Warren. Aleki and my father have some business to sort out, but I'm here for the food. Would you like to get some?"

"Some what?"

"Food. You can't attend an Avalian event and not eat. We pride ourselves on being hospitable. Not eating the food at a Pacific gathering is akin to kicking Queen Elizabeth in the crotch when you meet her. Come." Stella let herself be steered towards the long tables laden with delicacies.

Piling two plates full, Manu handed her one and promptly began chowing down on shrimp from his own plate.

Surveying her options, most of which were discouraged

by pregnancy blogs or had a high chance of leaving food in her teeth, Stella selected a tiny coconut cream tartlet from the plate. She bit into it, and moaned in satisfaction as the velvety filling spread across her tongue.

"This is amazing."

"I love those," Manu grinned at her around a mouthful of grilled pineapple. Stella smiled back affectionately. He was like a big puppy, all eyes, teeth and stomach. Glancing around the room, she caught sight of Aleki, deep in conversation with the Tongan princess. Her amusement evaporated as she watched him gesticulate. He hadn't even noticed she was gone. Unease built further, starting in her stomach and reaching up into her chest.

Is this what it's going to be like? Hanging out at the buffet watching other people mingle? I could get that by staying in New Zealand planning other people's weddings.

"Hey." A soft touch on her elbow made her jump.

Manu smiled at her gently. "You want to dance?"

Stella nodded, trying to push away the misery at the edges of her consciousness. Aleki's words came back to her.

It is essential that we present ourselves well tonight.

Realistically, she knew that hiding in the bathroom was not the way to show the gathered dignitaries that they were a strong unit. And if Aleki was too busy to dance with her, she would certainly accept the offer from someone else. The art of dance in Polynesia was highly regarded, and the best way for her to show her eagerness to embrace her baby's culture was to start assimilating as quickly as possible.

They were almost at the dancefloor when Tama intercepted them.

"Manu."

"Father." Manu inclined his head.

The king's eyes skipped over her. "Ms Warren." The greeting was lackluster, but in English.

She bowed. "King Tama." She switched to Avalian. "Thank you for your hospitality."

Tama's eyes darted back to her, shrewd and assessing. He nodded briefly, then said something she couldn't understand in Avalian to Manu and walked away. They carried on to the dancefloor in front of the dais where she and Aleki had sat at Tama's feet the day she arrived.

"How familiar are you with our language?" Manu spun her in a tight circle, pulling her back into a classic European dance position. He was careful to keep an appropriate amount of space between their bodies she noted.

Stella side eyed him, looking for a hint of jest under that perfect skin.

"A little. I'm learning as fast as I can but I'm afraid I still have a long way to go."

"We take the naming of our children seriously here on Avali. Meanings are ascribed, ancestors honoured. It's a whole thing. Literally translated, Manu means 'bird'. But the word itself is also used to communicate the ideas of strength and freedom. These are important concepts here. They encompass a great deal of the Avali spirit."

"And Aleki's name?"

Manu grinned quickly, a flash of white in a sea of bronze and Stella heard a stifled feminine moan from somewhere behind her.

"Aleki's name means 'defender'. He is the oldest, of course. It's his job to protect our people, our interests, our way of life. It's a heavy burden. And now he has someone to share it with."

"He's not really a sharer. And I'm not exactly equipped."

Manu threw his head back and laughed. "You, Ms Warren, are exactly what he needs."

"May I cut in?" The low voice reached inside Stella and melted the very parts she'd been trying to ice over.

"Well I don't know," Manu twirled her and her over-heated business around and dipped her quickly. "Does the lady want to dance with you?"

Aleki damn near growled. "She's my fiancée."

"And yet, you've ignored her all night." Another spin. "Maybe she's enjoying having someone pay a little attention to her."

Stella's stomach hurled itself against her admittedly weak abdominal muscles as she waited for Aleki's response.

"I've been *working*." Aleki's voice was tight, his eyes flashing fire that betrayed his anger. "It would be a lot easier if I wasn't the only one doing the bloody job. Maybe if you spent a little less time chasing a fucking ball around-"

"Hey, hey, hey." Manu cut in, standing straighter. His arms turned to stone under his shirt. "You didn't seem to mind me chasing fucking balls when it paid for the new science wing at the university."

"Okay." Stella stepped back. "That's enough, gentlemen. This is not the time, nor the place to be measuring your penile gifts from God. Manu," she extended her hand to her dance partner, "it was lovely to meet you. I hope to see you again soon."

Relaxing slightly, Aleki's younger brother lifted her hand and brushed his lips over the back of it. "Ms Warren, it was a pleasure and a delight. I wish you all the best." He turned towards his brother. "I'll see you later?"

Aleki gave a small nod, and accepted the departing slap on his chest stoically.

Stella reached out and linked her fingers through his.

They parted slowly, the strong digits like stones that hers needed to wiggle through.

"I missed you." The admission burned in her chest, vulnerability burrowing through the words.

"I had to work. It is rare to have this many dignitaries from across the Pacific in one place." His fingers tightened around hers. "You seemed well entertained."

His gaze didn't meet hers. He was focused on a group of older men near the banquet table.

"Sure. It was super entertaining listening to other women rip me apart in the toilets."

Aleki snorted, distracted by the group across the floor. "And I'm sure they regretted it. That's why I chose you, Stella. You don't need me to fight your battles for you." He motioned to the men by the suckling pigs. "Excuse me, little star. I have some business I need to attend to with the President of Kiribati."

Coldness seeped through Stella. She reached out and grabbed his hand. The electric energy that always accompanied Aleki's touch vibrated through her, but couldn't dislodge the icy grip of fear on her heart.

"You cut in just so you could leave me alone before the song finished? Aleki." She waited until his eyes met hers. "I'm tired. I'd like to leave soon."

She saw it flash across his face, the hunger, before he wrestled it down. Pasting on a patient look, he cajoled her. "Stella, I can't leave. You can wait for me in the parlour, or Andreas can drive you home and come back for me."

"Why can't you come now?" Her voice was strangled, but she ignored it, searching his face for any sign of reprieve.

He cares about you, you're important to him, he told you so.

"I'll be there soon, little star. But I must secure the

support I need here tonight. This deal is more important than anything else right now."

His words hung in the air in front of her, taunting her with its superiority. Flashes of memories she thought she had buried hit hard, looking for her father in a crowd, her hair in a tight bun and stage makeup caked across her watering eyes when she realised he wasn't there, even though he'd promised - *promised* - he'd come to this one. *Was your dance recital tonight? Oh well, your mum was there. It wasn't really that important, was it?* The ice that had gripped her earlier tightened around her limbs even as flames licked through the hollowness of her stomach. Nausea rose in her throat, not the empty vapour of her pregnancy but hot thick bile, a vicious yellow that swam at the edge of her consciousness even as she felt Aleki lift her hand to his lips for a kiss. Then he was gone, striding off towards the stupid men by their stupid pigs. And she was by herself, a trivial, insignificant afterthought recounting each and every mistake that had led her here again. But not alone. She wasn't alone, because her baby was with her. Her precious baby that she would lay down her life to protect from ever feeling this way.

The desperation to be somewhere - anywhere - else built, fighting the bile for influence as she marched down the corridor towards the main door. Battling the urge to run, she whipped her head around to search for Andreas the instant she felt the warm island air hit her face.

He was seated with a number of other drivers on the wide palace porch, playing cards to a background of ukulele and raucous joking. As soon as their eyes met though, he stood and started towards her. Another driver claimed his hand to slow him, but he shook the other man off and said something without ever taking his gaze off her face.

"Ms Warren?"

"Andreas." Her voice was shaky, weak, and she hated herself for it.

Stop it! Never show them how much you hurt. She made a concerted effort to strengthen her tone.

"I need to leave now."

THIRTEEN

Aleki stormed up the stairs and threw open Stella's door. The knob bounced off the drywall and the entire thing ricocheted back at him until the flat of his hand settled it back against the wall. Every ounce of frustration he'd wrestled on the long, lonely car ride home swarmed under his skin, his hand practically vibrating against the smooth wood.

"What the hell?" Stella's bedside light flipped on as she turned towards him.

"Oh. It's you." Her unenthusiastic announcement enraged him further.

"What are you playing at Stella? I was very clear that we needed to make a good impression tonight. How do you think it looks to have me wandering around trying to find my fiancée?"

"I don't know," she snapped, her gaze narrowing on him from across the room. "Why don't you ask the President of Kiribati? He seemed to have a lot of thoughts."

Frustration propelled him forward until he was standing at the side of the bed he'd come to think of as theirs. "Is that what this is about? You're mad I didn't pay enough attention to you, so you left?"

She lifted her chin and the full brunt of her glare hit him. It was the first time she'd ever aimed her fighting eyes directly at him and his stomach curdled, even as he noted the reddened rims and swollen skin around them.

"Enough attention?" she scoffed. "I could have been a fucking wall hanging for all you noticed. Tell me, Aleki, how long did it take you to realise I was gone? An hour? Two?"

He wrested away the seed of guilt that sprung up at her accusation, because truthfully it had been close to the latter, and focused on his anger.

"That's not the point! We were supposed to be a united front."

"How united could we be if we barely actually spoke to one another once we walked in? Do you think people didn't notice that *before* I left, Aleki? Don't blame me for not putting on a show of shining coupledom if all you wanted was someone to follow you around like a silent puppy."

"All I wanted," he stressed through gritted teeth, "was to complete the business I needed to. "

"And you did or you wouldn't be here, so good for you. But your needs don't get to be more important than mine through an accident of birth, Aleki. You might be a prince, but you're still a person, the same as me. And as a *person*, I needed my fiancé to take care of me in a new and strange social setting. You know, the way you promised you would on our way in."

"You can take care of yourself." He waved a hand as if to dismiss her complaint. Stella was the most capable woman he knew, except for perhaps Lani.

Stella blinked up at him, the slow, heavy struggle of her lashes belying the tears that swam in her eyes.

"Of course I can take care of myself." Her voice cracked and she winced at the show of weakness. "But I don't want to just slot into your life when it's convenient for you, Aleki. I don't want that for our child, either. And I'm terrified that will happen. You'll get so caught up in your own life that we'll become an afterthought."

"How can you think that?"

"It happens all the time, Aleki." Stella's voice was small, pleading. "Women and children left at home, waiting for their partners and parents to come home. Waiting to feel like they matter. Like spending time with them takes priority over deals and parties and God-knows-what."

Intellectually Aleki knew she was speaking from experience - from the little girl inside her who never felt like her father had loved her enough, but the fire born of Pacific pride burned within him at the suggestion that he might be found lacking. The flames of his ego licked high within him, almost blocking out the haze of fear that she might be right. That maybe he couldn't do this role justice. That perhaps he might fail as a father as spectacularly as he was failing at being a prince.

"I will be the best father," he declared, putting enough force behind the words to convince anyone listening. "I am not Graham. I will not forget birthdays and leave our baby at a damn racetrack." The tidbits of information he'd learned from Luke about Stella's father flowed out on a tide of resentment.

Stella visibly flinched at his words, tugging the blanket tighter around her like a protective cocoon.

"Maybe not," she conceded softly. "But will you make sure they feel important? Will you make sure *I* feel important to you? You told me this would be a real marriage and I've worked hard to believe you. It's not easy for me to think about giving up my business, my dreams to come here and live when I know nobody else. But partners in a real marriage support each other. They care about each other. And I thought we could have that together."

"We can."Aleki cried. "But tonight was not the night to test that, Stella. You have no idea what kind of pressure I'm under."

"How can I, if you won't *tell* me?" She lowered her eyes to the quilt, picking at a corner, her voice a violent mix of frustration and despair. "For God's sake Aleki, *talk* to me. We're supposed to be a team, but all you've done tonight is shut me out."

"You wouldn't understand." He spat the words, watching as each one hit her like a barb. "My entire life, everything I've worked for is on the line now. If I can't make this one deal happen, Manu will become the heir to Avali. I won't have a kingdom. I won't even have a job."

"Why didn't you say so?"

 "Because the only thing I needed from you tonight was to stand beside me and smile. I thought you'd be able to manage that, but apparently not."

He knew immediately that he'd crossed the line. Stella's perfect, tear-streaked face iced over as his words registered, a terrible coldness radiating out from her like an arctic wave. He took another step closer to the bed but she stopped him, her palm stretched out to ward him off. Fear twisted his gut, pushing air from his lungs that coiled up his windpipe, knotting in the back of his throat. She raised her eyes to his and his anxiety cemented itself at the glacial remoteness in her gaze. He knew that look. He'd seen it before, whenever she talked about her father. The man who had constantly let her down.

His mouth dry, he tried to scramble the words back. "Stel-"

"Leave." Hard. Dispassionate. Her tone matched her features, carved in stone, divorced from the funny, spirited woman he'd licked to orgasm mere hours ago.

And because he was a coward, he did.

———

STELLA HELD herself together just long enough to hear Aleki shut the door behind him and his soft footfalls drift down the stairs. Then she broke. Hot tears sluiced down her cheeks in a waterfall, unchecked as she gasped air in hulking sobs. The burn of rejection spread through her, lighting up every nerve ending with her inadequacy. And through all the pain, a tiny voice whispered into the back of her brain.

You knew you could never be enough.

And wasn't that the pure, sickening truth of it. She was never enough. Not for Aleki, who needed a royal bride, one who would be an asset not a liability. Not for her father, whose desire for a son overshadowed every achievement she'd strived for in a never ending quest for his approval. Not even for her mother, who had died alone at home, Stella's need for her no match for the cancer that had stolen through her undetected until it was too late because Mary Warren didn't want to bother the doctor with her unexplained bruises and vomiting.

The abandonment she'd felt earlier at the ball pulsed inside her again, louder than before, edged with the sharp pain of self-disgust. She knew love. She'd built her career, her *life*, around love, yet here she was again, swimming in the dredges of almost-enough while her heart called out to someone who didn't want the real her.

Pathetic.

Enough was enough. She breathed deeply, held it for five seconds then exhaled.

In and out. In and out. In and out.

Once she'd wrangled her respiratory system back under control, she tossed back the covers and padded across the cool tile to the en suite to wash away the sticky heat of humiliation. She might not be loveable, but she could damn well do her job. And for the next three days, her job was to be the best fiancée the Avalian royal family had ever seen. Just three days left of her trial visit and she could go home, back to the safety of her black-and-white apartment, her spreadsheets and lists, her orderly life. There would be time to discuss their situation after she returned to Wellington. To establish expectations and boundaries, and get a contract signed. No matter what Aleki had said her first day here, this visit had shown that she could not keep her feelings contained while they played house like messy toddlers, roaming the gauntlet of a real relationship without considering the consequences. It would be much better to craft an official business relationship. No sex. No easy dinners in the courtyard. A marriage in name only. The way it should have been all along.

Stella twisted the shower on, continuing her breathing exercises while she ran through the to-do list in her head as she waited for the water to warm up.

Contact lawyer for contract - not Luke's brother! Maybe set fire to Luke's brother's car. Check Aleki's schedule for a visit to New Zealand around the due date. Start looking for a two-bedroom apartment.

She stripped off her clothes thoughtlessly, her mind humming with minutiae to distract her from the yawning hole in her chest. After sticking one hand in the water to test the temperature, she bundled her hair into a makeshift bun and hooked her fingers into the sides of the underwear she'd pulled on the instant she got back to the house. Peeling them down her legs, she focused on her breath, *in and out, in and out, in and out.*

And then she saw the blood.

FOURTEEN

Weariness stole across Aleki's shoulders, settling around him like a blanket. Even in the violet light of dawn, the promise of another beautiful day lingered in the heaviness of the air, the warm whisper of the breeze through the coconut palms that lined his driveway. It did nothing to alleviate the tension bunching his muscles tighter than the strings on a fresh ukelele. Each step away from his truck towards the villa balcony bathed in gold light felt like a step towards the gallows.

Stella would be pissed off. There was no getting around it. Last night, in the little *fale* in the bush, he'd tossed and turned in the bed that suddenly felt too big, examining the events of the ball and their fight after from every angle.

He'd been wrong. Even now, the realisation hit a bum note, clanging uncomfortably within him. Stella was nothing but an asset in every facet of his life, and ignoring her at the ball when he should have been celebrating her, letting her shine so that the strength of Avali's future was apparent in every flash of her smile and squeeze of their hands would have done more to soothe the ruffled political feathers in the room than his desperate attempts to secure support.

Doubling down in her bedroom by implying she was nothing more than a pretty face was simply the act of an imbecile.

No, he had no doubt she planned to make him pay for her forgiveness.

I'll make it up to her, he vowed as he reached the carved door. *The next three days before she leaves will be the best of her life.*

Determination gave his push of the door an extra edge and he entered the foyer to see Lani scrambling off a low bench by the stairs, straightening her skirt as she stood.

"Lani?"

"Your Highness." She bowed her head.

"What are you doing here? You don't start until seven."

Lani bit her lip, a faint blush painting her cheeks a copper shade as her eyes darted between him and the floor.

"Is it Pania? Did you have a fight?"

"No, sir." She took a deep breath and focused her gaze on him. "It's Ms Warren."

Aleki winced. "How angry is she? What should I prepare for?" Because there was no question that Lani would not have stayed the night for just any angry girl he left behind.

"You don't need to prepare for anything. She's gone."

Time stopped. His breath soured in his lungs, twining up his esophagus and squeezing the oxygen from his body in a gasp. The sluggish beat of his heart echoed in his ears, loud enough to drown out Lani as she stepped closer to him. Her mouth was moving, but he couldn't register anything over the dull thump-thump-thump that pounded through his head.

"What about Monday?" Aleki blurted. "She's supposed to stay until Monday."

Lani paused and took him by the elbow, leading him over to the bench she'd been resting on while clearly waiting for his return. He allowed himself to be led like a lamb, settled on the plush seat before she continued.

"Yes, she was supposed to stay until Monday." Lani said gently, slowly. "But there was a complication. She had some bleeding, and we had to call the doctor."

Aleki whipped his head around, fear clutching at him.

"The baby?" *Gods, no, not our baby.*

"The baby is fine," Lani hurried to reassure him. "The doctor checked Ms Warren thoroughly. There was a strong heartbeat and no other signs of concern. She mentioned that sometimes in the first trimester there can be a little blood, but she didn't see any reason to worry. Ms Warren also indicated she would be seeing her own specialist as soon as she returned home."

"I don't understand." The panic that had held him hostage since he walked in was receding, leaving a rising wave of anger in its wake. "Why would she leave? If she were concerned about the baby and only had three days remaining in her stay, why creep away in the middle of the night?"

Discomfort played across Lani's full mouth. "She, uh, she seemed to make the decision after being unable to get hold of you when the doctor left. She tried to call you as soon as the doctor had been summoned but after several hours without an answer, she decided to leave."

Aleki stared at her for a beat, then yanked his phone from his pocket.

Thirty-seven notifications. Missed calls and texts from Stella, Lani and Andreas. Hours worth of aborted attempts to reach him. The last one was from Andreas thirty minutes ago, confirming he'd escorted Stella to the airport and watched her board the early flight safely.

He sagged back against the wall.

"I was at the fale in the valley." His voice was hollow. "No reception. And my phone was on silent when I came back out."

Lani rubbed his shoulder gently, a maternal gesture.

"Would you like me to arrange a flight for you?"

"It won't help." Aleki was sure of that. "We had a fight after the ball. I treated her poorly. Stella won't have any desire to see me at the moment." A frustrated sigh squeezed from his chest. "Perhaps it's better if I just let her cool off." He rose wearily to his feet.

"Thank you for your help, Lani. You're a good friend. Please take the rest of the weekend off. Give all staff the rest of the weekend off. I'll see you on Monday."

He trudged up the stairs and down the hallway, the yawning hole his chest tightening as he passed the closed door to Stella's room. He made it to the master suite and kicked off his shoes, each one landing with a soft thump against the wall. Undoing his cufflinks, he tossed himself on the bed then turned to place them on his nightstand when he saw the folded paper.

Jackknifing up, he reached for the note.

Aleki,

You're not answering your phone and I don't have another way to get hold of you. Lani's tried as well. The doctor was here earlier - there was some bleeding but she assures me the baby is fine. I've decided to leave early to return to New Zealand. Not because of the baby, though I'll be happy to see my own specialist. I'm leaving because this isn't working. The lines between us have become blurred. I keep forgetting what it is you want from me, and I can't keep pretending what I want isn't important. The truth is, I want someone who I can call to be there in the middle of the night for me. Not just for the baby, but for me. You can't give me that and it's not fair of me to ask you to put aside your work for a sham of a marriage. So I think it's better if we call the whole thing off. I'd rather our child grow up with happy co-parents than in an unhappy marriage. I left the ring in my room. I'll be in touch soon to hash out the details of the coming months.

Stella.

There it was. In black and white. He couldn't give her what she wanted. As if a house, a husband, a baby and a title wasn't enough. The anger started slowly, rolling to a boil as he read and reread the words. Maybe she was right, perhaps they were better off apart. But dammit, she should have spoken to him about it. Not snuck out in the night like a thief, leaving him alone in this big house without her laugh, or her lists or the slight firmness of her tummy where his *pepe* grew.

Now it was just him. No staff. No family. Just a man without a fiancée. At least he had his liquor cabinet.

It was time to get very, very drunk.

———

"ALEKI?"

Someone was calling his name from very far away. Aleki tried to groan in response but nothing came out. He swallowed thickly, his throat like sandpaper and tried again.

"Unf."

It was enough. Footsteps sounded around his head and

he heard the soft swish of the curtains being opened. A shaft of light softened the dullness behind his closed lids. He struggled to open his eyes but gave it up as a lost cause when it caused the pain in his temples to radiate like the sun.

"Gods." Manu sounded amused. The bastard. "You look like shit."

Aleki summoned every particle of strength in his body and, concentrating very carefully, flipped the bird in the direction of his brother's voice.

"Now, now," the cocky voice chided in Avalian. "That's not nice. Especially when I brought you the elixir of life."

Aleki valiantly tried to open his eyes again, and his success was rewarded with blinding agony.

"Here." A bottle of water was shoved into one hand, and a couple of small tablets into the other. "Take these."

"Why are you here?" He tossed the pills in his mouth and swallowed half the water in a single swallow.

"You missed church."

Fuck. The photo op of him, Manu and the king attending a Sunday service had been organised by Iosefa and emailed out on Friday evening. He'd seen it while flipping through his notifications on Saturday morning before the tequila took total control.

"Is Dad mad?"

Manu shrugged. "When is he not?"

Aleki raised an eyebrow in acknowledgement and tipped the bottle to his lips to swallow the remaining liquid.

"So," Manu looked around, taking in the empty bottles that littered Stella's -*his spare guest* - room. "Where is the delightful Ms Warren?"

"Gone."

"Just like that?"

"Yup." Aleki crumpled the water bottle in his hand, frowning viciously at it.

"Hmmm." Manu's tone was indecipherable, but Aleki couldn't be bothered looking up to determine his meaning. "What did you do?"

At that, his head shot up. "What makes you think I did something? Maybe she just doesn't want this life. Maybe she--" he hesitated "--maybe she just doesn't want me."

His brother snorted. "Yeah, women hate princes. They make films about it all the time."

"It's not that."

"So what is it?"

"It's complicated. The wedding, the relationship." He took a deep breath. "Stella's pregnant."

"No way?" Manu's face lit up like he'd just been handed a ten-year rugby league contract. "I'm going to be an uncle?"

"There's more. I asked her to marry me for the baby's sake. I can't take another scandal. I was very clear, there was even a contract at one point. Stella agreed for her own reasons. And now she's gone. She thinks we'd be better as co-parents." He infused the last world with all the bitterness that simmered under the surface of his skin.

"And you can't get her back?"

Aleki gave a hollow laugh. "She doesn't want me. She wants a father for her child, but not me as such. And anyway-" he swallowed thickly around the lie, "--I don't want her like that."

"Bullshit," Manu laughed. "Men don't spend two days drunk because their fake fiancée leaves them. They do when their real one does, though."

Aleki groaned and rolled over onto his stomach.

"So if you're not getting her back, what are you going to do?"

"The only thing I can do." The pillow muffled his voice so he turned his head, inhaling a quick, dizzying hit of Stella's perfume from the cushion. "I'm going to do my job. I'm going to secure the Samoan trade deal and reclaim my rightful place as heir from you."

"I don't know." Manu's cheerfulness suddenly sounded forced. "I might as well lead the country. I've got nothing else going on."

"What about the league season?"

"They're releasing me from my contract." His little brother's voice suddenly sounded smaller. "I'm still having some injury trouble and the club didn't take kindly to me jumping on a plane this week to check on you."

"You don't have leave?" Shock raced across Aleki's skin, leaving goosebumps in its wake. "Manu! Why would you risk something like that?"

Manu rolled his eyes, exasperation carved in every inch of his face. "For you, you idiot. You get engaged out of the blue, to a foreign girl we've never heard of, and I find out about it on the news? Of course I came to check on you."

Guilt weighed heavy on Aleki's shoulders, pressing against the uncomfortable shard of grief that always pinched in his chest when he thought about what his actions had cost his brother.

"You have to go back, Manu. You can't risk your career for me. Not again." The pressure built, a pointed tip that burrowed deeper down, crippling in its intensity.

"Hey, hey, hey." Manu was by his side, kneeling on the tiles. "What do you mean, not again?"

"The accident," Aleki gasped out, rubbing his fist against the radiating pain in his chest. "You almost lost it all after the accident. Now you're risking it again. No matter what I do, I keep putting your job in jeopardy."

"Is that what you think? You think you're responsible for my accident? For my choices?" Manu sighed. "I'm twenty-five years old, Aleki. I make my own decisions. And I decided my family took priority over playing this week. I knew what the consequences might be, and I still got on that plane. And the accident was years ago. You didn't cause it. Hell, I didn't even know where you were when it happened. Tua and I could have made a million different decisions that day, and maybe he'd still be here and maybe my knee would be alright but maybe things would have gone the way they did anyway. We'll never know." He shrugged. "But what I do know is that it's time to stop blaming yourself for what happened to other people. You're the best brother I could ask for. And I bet you'd be a pretty good husband too if you could stop blaming yourself for Stella's choices."

FIFTEEN

"Why don't you love me?"

"It's not a matter of not loving you. An eighteen-foot-long flower wall isn't in our budget."

Stella suppressed the eye roll that would threaten her contract with the recently engaged couple sitting on the other side of her desk and interrupted.

"Perhaps we could come back to the decor later? Which cake flavour is your favourite so far?"

"I like the lemon," the groom-to-be said, bravely ignoring the daggers his future wife was staring into his temple.

"Gina?"

"The lemon's fine."

"Fabulous." Stella beamed at the couple and set down her own fork on the plate of cake samples. "So, a three-tier lemon cake with blueberry mousse and a white-chocolate ganache. And the chocolate cupcakes as an alternative to the groom's cake. Shall we move on to the invitation suite?"

By the time her office door closed behind the bickering couple, Stella was exhausted. Some events were a walk in the park, but some she could tell from the outset would be trouble. Gina-and-Brandtly's wedding was one, and she'd bet a reasonable chunk of her fee they'd be divorced within five years. Since her scare in Avali, she was having a harder than usual time keeping her own feelings under the surface. The reality of lying alone under the stark, assessing gaze of a doctor while he prodded at her before declaring the bleeding inconsequential had frightened her more than she'd realised at the time. She'd spent more than one night trembling with a head full of what-ifs and the dawning understanding that this would be what her entire foray into motherhood would be. Her and her baby, a team against the world. Lying her head on her desk she breathed deeply, resting a hand on her stomach. The firmness of her slightly swollen belly under her white silk blouse made her smile, and she gave it a gentle rub.

I'll take care of you, little one. We'll be fine.

"Hey, Stella? I'm going to lunch. Do you want me to grab you anything?" Her assistant, Jessie, popped her head around the door.

"Maybe a steak and cheese pie?"

"Done." Jessie gave her a funny look on her way out of the office.

Stella shook her head a little and turned back towards her computer. Leaning back in her ergonomic chair, she flipped open the Gina-and-Brandtly's Doomed Wedding binder and scanned the contents. Jessie had taken the booking while she was in the islands, and the March date gave Stella pause. She was due in March, and currently had no idea how she would manage an events business nine months pregnant, let alone post-partum. A partnership was the obvious solution, but rebranding would be a nightmare and it would only be successful if she could find the right colleague to help her juggle her work-life balance once the baby arrived. Especially if she'd be traveling to Avali regularly so her child could spend time with its father.

The thought of Aleki still stung, but in the fortnight since she'd fled Avali the pain had receded to a point where her breath no longer caught in her chest when she thought of him. Two weeks of deafening silence had done more to disillusion her to the idea that he might have feelings for her than any of the things he'd said during their final night together.

Her own stupidity though, in falling for a man who had quite clearly said and shown that he had no interest in romantic relationships, was still a sore point. One that she hugged to her chest in the dark at night, a gaping wound where hope used to reside.

On impulse, she picked up the phone and dialled his number.

"Fa'alofa?"

Just for a second, her heart stopped, the rich timbre of his accent pouring through her like sunshine.

"Aleki. It's, uh, it's Stella."

A pause. "Stella."

"Yes. I, um, I'm just calling about the baby." She rolled her eyes, both at the lame excuse and her mangled delivery.

"Is everything alright?"

"Yes. I just wanted to check in. Did you get the results email from the specialist?"

"I did." He sounded... careful. As though her question might be a trap.

"So, the bleeding can be common in the first trimester. I've just entered the second now so there's a much lower chance of miscarriage from here on out."

"I'm glad to hear that."

Giving up on all hope of dignity, Stella breathed out her next sentence in a rush. "I, um, I wanted to apologise for the way I left things. It was unfair to you and I should have waited to speak to you personally."

A faint noise from the other end of the line - the slightest hitch of breath.

"Stel--"

She carried on, pushing through whatever he might try to say in her need to get the words out. "I really do want this to be fair for both of us. I've hired another lawyer to draft up a more equitable parental agreement since marriage is no longer on the table."

There was a long pause.

"A parenting agreement." Aleki's voice was tight. "I see. If that's what you want, of course I'll sign. Have the documents sent to Lani. Is there anything else?"

The last vestiges of optimism withered inside her. Cold seeped through the hole it left, freezing her slowly from her bones out.

"Uh, no." She shook her head slowly, tears pricking at the backs of her eyes. "No, I'll let you get back to whatever it is you're doing."

"Okay, take care." The dial tone rang in her ear, a flat chord that sounded just like the final sound of a heart monitor. *Ironic*, she thought, as she lowered her phone to the desk, the pain in her own heart a nuclear explosion mushrooming out over the numbness of her surrounding body.

The sound of her office door brought her back to the present, and she fought through the fog in her head to say something, anything, that would sound normal and also ensure she was left alone.

"Can you grab me a chocolate milk too, Jessie?"

"Pardon?"

Startling at the unfamiliar voice, Stella swiveled in her chair.

"What are you doing here?"

Tala Tuila cleared her throat and shifted her weight between her feet.

"I'd like to speak to you."

"I don't know that we have anything to discuss." The memory of Aleki's broken confession following their televised interview broke through her own heartbreak and hardened her voice.

"Well, I'd like to apologise then." Tala entered and sat in the chair Jessie had recently vacated. "I acted poorly towards you in Avali and I'm sorry for that."

Suspicion kept Stella from replying. Tala's eyes darted towards her left hand before returning to her eyes. "You're not wearing your engagement ring."

Stella let the silence swell into discomfort that hung thick in the space between them.

Tala closed her eyes briefly and exhaled.

"My job is not easy. I'm young and I'm a woman. In Avali, that means I have to work four times as hard to be taken half as seriously by the public and my colleagues. The interview with you and Prince Aleki was an opportunity to assert myself as more of a hard-hitting journalist, and I took it."

"Was it worth it?"

"Yes." Tala's reply was quick and adamant. "I'm in Wellington today as a foriegn correspondent covering your election and the impact it will have on the relationship between our countries. It's a trial assignment to gauge my potential for a shift to the evening news."

A small smile twisted Stella's lips. "That's a great opportunity."

"It is. I'm not sorry for trying to establish myself in my career, but I do want to apologise for ambushing you and for any problems that may have caused between yourself and His Highness. It wasn't fair to you and it certainly wasn't in keeping with the hospitality of our country."

The small coil of anger unfurled in Stella's stomach as she considered the younger woman. Wanting to succeed was certainly a familiar notion, and resenting Tala for taking the chance to further her career with their disastrous interview sat uncomfortably with her.

"Okay," she said at last. "I accept your apology. Thank you for taking the time to come and deliver it in person. I wish you all the best in your career."

Tala smiled briefly, a glint of determination evident in her dark eyes.

"Actually, Ms Warren, there is one other thing."

ALEKI SANK UNCEREMONIOUSLY into his desk chair, exhaustion making his muscles dense and his movements ungainly. The soft cushioning embraced him, giving him a single glorious moment of respite before he flipped open the lid of his laptop and the blue glow of responsibility shone out at him from the screen. Navigating to his emails, he skipped past several regarding upcoming school visits and focused instead on the ones from Avali's minister for trade, outlining the finalised details of the Samoa deal that both countries had signed the week before.

Relief poured through him. It was done. His position was secure. Parliament could take care of the rest, but he, Prince Aleki, had fulfilled his promise to his king and secured a measure of economic stability for his people.

If only he could be happy about it.

He took comfort in the knowledge, certainly. The signing had lifted his own burden, but also that of the farmers and suppliers. Yet the hollowness in his chest had not abated. If anything, it was deeper, darker, more tangled since Stella's phone call.

A new parental agreement, her words echoed in his head. *Since marriage is no longer on the table*.

If he'd harbored any hope that she was calling to restore their relationship, those words had shot it dead. The best thing he could do now was to honour her request.

A knock at the door pulled his attention from the screen. Lani entered his office, bearing his lunch tray.

"Good afternoon."

"Lani." He watched as she lowered the tray to his desk. Chop suey, fried chicken and taro leaves poached in coconut milk. Comfort food.

"Thank you." He offered a weary smile up at her. "I appreciate your hard work."

Lani smiled back, a cautious pull of her lips that immediately put him on guard.

"Is there something wrong?"

His assistant sighed. "May I speak plainly?"

"You usually do." He gestured to the vacant chairs in front of his desk.

She sank gracefully into one, holding his gaze. "I'm worried about you. We all are. You've been working so hard recently, and doing far more than I've scheduled. I know the Samoa deal was important to you, but it's done now. Yet you spent all this week in meetings with the tourism minister, the finance minister and the Parliament sitting going over referendum options. You visited farms and hospitals and parent groups. All spontaneous, unscheduled visits. You haven't eaten, you haven't rested. Even on Sundays you are out with the people. That is not a healthy life, sir. Without taking some time to yourself, you will have nothing of yourself left to offer."

"Lani, I am heir to the throne of Avali. My focus should always be on our people. On their governance, yes, but also on their lives. The day-to-day life of the villagers, the fisheries, the farmers and the industrial workers. I have been distracted before now, and I have neglected my duties. I am determined to do better."

Lani hesitated. "But what about your duty to your family?"

Righteous indignation swelled. "I *am* doing my duty to my family," he snapped. "The king asked me to complete the Samoa deal, and I have. He asks that I focus on our infrastructure, and I have. The Esera family has ruled Avali for almost three hundred years. I will not be the leader that lets our country fall behind the rest of the Pacific during my reign. That means I need to work harder, work longer than my predecessors. The years that I spent travelling and living an aimless life full of parties and frivolity were years where I could have been properly preparing to lead. It was selfish of me not to think of my people then. I will not make that mistake again."

"The king and Manu are not your only family," Lani shot back. "Your child will need you too."

"My child is not here yet," Aleki raged. "My child's mother wants nothing to do with me. The harder I work now, the better life I will be able to provide for my son or daughter. How dare you question my loyalty to my child! They will have a father - a ruler - to be proud of."

"Are you proud of yourself?"

Hot anger pulsed through him in waves. "You forget your place, Lani. Shut the door behind you."

Lani's eyes dropped immediately. In all their years together he had never rebuked her such.

"Yes, sir." Her normally strong voice was small. "Forgive me. I will check on you again before I leave for the day." Standing, she moved swiftly to the door, the click of the latch slicing through the tension shimmering in the air.

Aleki sank back in his chair, breathing heavily. A pang of remorse sang through him. Of everyone, he knew that Lani only wanted the best for him. The whole time they had worked together she had always put his needs first. Yet still the weight of unyielding expectation lay on him like a rock. His father, his people, Lani, his unborn child.

When will it be enough?

Once more, his thoughts drifted to his final fight with Stella. The things they'd said, flinging hurt on both sides. He'd replayed it in his mind over and over, examining it from all angles, picking it apart like an equation to be solved. The thing was, he couldn't solve it. The phone call he'd received from her only served to highlight the gulf between them. He'd been so surprised to hear her voice and desperate not to break down and beg down the line for her return that he'd come across as an uncommunicative asshole. Now, as he sat stewing in guilt about the way he'd snapped at Lani, he could see why.

Words meant nothing. Not to someone like Stella, who had been lied to or her father all her life. Actions spoke louder, and the action he'd taken so far only showed that he didn't care enough to make room for her in his life.

Grinding his molars against the thought, he pressed the button that would summon Lani to his office.

"Sir?"

Contrition walloped him again as he took in the way Lani peeped around the door, the waver in her voice.

"Lani. Come in, come in." He waited until she was seated before continuing. "I would like to offer my apologies. My actions were atrocious as an employer and inexcusable as a friend. I am sorry."

He held his breath until Lani offered a small nod, then exhaled in relief. "Thank you. And thank you for working with me during this time."

"It has not been the easiest period of my employment," his assistant acknowledged wryly. "But I'm sure it will get better soon."

Aleki huffed out a laugh. "I hope so. That was the other thing I wanted to talk to you about." He hesitated, the words playing on the tip of his tongue until he gathered the courage to spit them out, quickly like they'd mean less if they were said at great speed. "It's come to my attention that I do not handle conflict well. And I was wondering if you could arrange someone for me to talk to. About that." He shifted in his seat, pinpricks of discomfort swarming under his skin as he stared directly at his laptop screen to avoid seeing any kind of pity or judgement in Lani's eyes.

"Of course." Her answer was warm. "There's a wonderful man I know who helped me when I was planning on coming out to my parents. Would you like me to see if he's available?"

"Yes, please." Aleki risked a glance at his assistant, and the pride in her eyes almost knocked the breath from him.

"Any preference for times?"

He shrugged. "You know my schedule better than I do. Just, um-" He cleared his throat, knocking away the lump of anxiety that had been lodged there since Stella had left. "-

Maybe just if we could meet quite quickly? And quite regularly, to begin with."

Lani nodded, and rounding the desk, pulled him into a swift, powerful hug. Before he could raise his arms to embrace her as well, she pulled back, wiped a tear from her cheek and smacked him lightly on the shoulder.

"Eat your chicken."

Then she was gone, leaving behind the scent of coconut oil and the feeling that he was twenty kilograms lighter.

SIXTEEN

The early dawn light spilled through Aleki's study window as he put the finishing touches on the presentation for the Alternative Pathways Initiative before the Parliamentary session that began at nine. Despite his satisfaction with the programme and the opportunities it would offer Avali's young people, he still found himself fidgeting as he doctored the final format several times, trying to ensure it looked its best. He wouldn't be the one presenting it, but he desperately wanted it to impress. In the back of his mind, an eighteen-year-old Stella laughed as he fiddled with font choices.

Not Arial, Aleki! It's a default font! It makes it look like you don't care.

A restless few hours sleep had done nothing to soothe his whirring brain or fill the emptiness that echoed within him. Logically, he could acknowledge that the discomfort stemmed from Stella's departure, but logic did nothing to ease the resentment that pulsed in her wake. The last fortnight of daily therapy sessions had helped him come to terms with learning to feel the full force of his emotions instead of avoiding them. It didn't mean he had to like it though.

A sudden pounding at the front door startled him, and he moved to answer it, dragging a hand across his face in a futile attempt to wipe away his fatigue.

He opened the door to find Manu's hulking frame darkening his entranceway, clad in sweaty workout gear.

"There's a doorbell. You don't need to try and beat my door down with your ham-fists."

"Fuck off." Manu strode past him purposefully, heading towards the living quarters. "Have you been watching TV this morning?"

"Of course not. Some of us have jobs you know."

"I ran here." Manu's words floated back to him. "It's twenty kilometers. I'd like to see you work that hard."

Aleki followed Manu's voice and sank onto one of the low beige couches as his brother fiddled with the television remote.

"What are you doing?"

"You'll see."

Manu flicked through the local channels until Tala Tuila's face filled the huge screen.

"God, why that woman?" Aleki groaned, hugging a throw cushion to his chest. "You know how I feel about her."

"I know how you feel about all women," Manu replied evenly. "Coffee?"

"Yeah."

As his brother bustled into the kitchen, the whirr of the espresso machine and clink of cups drifting out, Aleki tried to focus on what Tala was saying rather

"And we have been lucky enough to obtain an interview with Prince Aleki's betrothed, Ms Stella Warren."

Aleki shot up, adrenaline gunning through him, his focus entirely on the screen.

Stella would never betray me like that! Not after he'd made his feelings about journalists perfectly clear. Yet there she was, calm and collected in white silk, her chestnut hair pulled back in a simple knot and pearls at her ears. He recognised the background as her office, where he'd spent half a day waiting while she worked to prepare for her hasty departure to Avali after his amateurish proposal. He soaked in the sight of her, a consummate professional in her element. Hunger and pain warred in his system without either gaining an advantage as his eyes took in the smooth tan of her skin, the perfect bow of her top lip, the dark smudges under her eyes that were the only hint of the pregnancy exhaustion he'd seen her battling day in and day out.

She was discussing the symbiotic tourism potential of wedding and honeymoon packages between New Zealand and the Pacific, and his chest wrenched with the reminder that he could already be on his honeymoon with this woman if he'd only made sure she knew how he felt before it was too late.

"Ms Warren." Tala's voice came from off camera, but the microphone positioned in front of Stella indicated the footage was not live. She'd been there. Stella had granted Tala an interview even knowing how he felt about her. Anger welled inside him, clashing with his other emotions.

"Your absence in Avali has caused some questions. Do you plan to return soon?"

"The intention was always for me to visit Avali for a short time while Prince Aleki and I worked out the details of our arrangement. I'm sure the Avali populace can understand that, as a small-business owner it would be remiss of me not to return to my staff and clients and honour my commitments to them."

"But you will be coming back?"

"I look forward to visiting Avali again soon."

Her answers were honest but non-committal and he felt a surge of pride at how well she was playing the game. She would have been an incredible princess.

"Are you and Prince Aleki still engaged?"

Stella gave the off-camera Tala a reproachful look. "I will not comment on my relationship status with Prince Aleki. It would be disrespectful to do so without his consent. I will say one thing though." She turned her attention towards the camera once more, and Aleki's breath caught in his chest as her arresting green eyes seemed to pin him in place through the screen. "Prince Aleki Esera is one of the best men I have ever met. He cares about his country and its people more than anything. I cannot think of anyone who would be more committed to their work and to the success of their nation than your prince. You are lucky to have him. Anyone would be lucky to have him."

The screen switched back to Tala but Aleki stayed hunched forward on the couch, the pillow clutched to his chest, Tala's speculation about the status of their relationship washing over him as his thoughts remained clinging to the image of Stella looking through to him and claiming that he cared more about Avali than anything.

Anything.

The thought rang in his head. *Is that what she thinks? That I hold my work in higher regard than her? Than the baby?*

The idea startled him into motion. He swung up from the couch and turned to see Manu leaning against the arch between the kitchen and living areas, regarding him over the rim of a white coffee cup.

"Hell of a woman, that."

"To talk to the press? I've had that kind of woman before. I don't need another one." The words came automatically but the anger he'd felt earlier had dissipated, leaving only the swirling maelstrom that had plagued him since the morning after the ball.

"Yeah? You don't need a woman who defends you? Talks you up? Tells the world you're worth a damn?"

Aleki didn't answer, his mind replaying the footage of Stella, beautiful, generous Stella, telling his people how lucky they were to have him. How lucky *anyone* would be to have him.

Anyone.

Like her.

Suddenly the emptiness that had dogged him for weeks made sense. It wasn't that Stella was missing from his home. It was that she was missing from his life. The niggle of uncertainty that had dogged him for weeks was the knowledge that he had failed her. Not the way he worried about failing his people, but as a friend. Certainly as a lover. When she had left, he'd been angry. Rather than stopping to consider the validity of her claims, he'd lashed out and run away. Just like last time he'd let someone down. And now? He'd spent a month sitting on his arse sulking because he was too scared to follow his heart and ask for her forgiveness. Too cowardly to put himself in a position to be told he wasn't good enough again. But there she was, on television, telling the whole world that he was. He was enough.

He could no longer let his cowardice stop him from the life he wanted to live. If that meant Tama gave the crown to Manu, so be it. He would still be a prince. He would still be able to serve his people. But maybe he would be able to do it with Stella by his side.

Still ignoring his brother, Aleki dug his cellphone out of his pocket and thumbed through to Andreas's number.

"Andreas? I need the car out front immediately. We're leaving early."

From the doorway Manu lifted an eyebrow. "I'll put this in a travel cup."

Minutes later, both armed with steaming travel cups, they piled into the back of Andreas's car. Aleki's leg knee shook up and down as they drove, nervous energy ricocheting through his system as the Parliamentary building grew closer.

Once seated, he stroked his fingers over the glossy wood of the head table positioned on the dais of the Avalian Parliment. Around him, the premier politicians who guided his country buzzed. Papers shuffled, allegiances shifted and the flag of Avali marched in rows along the rafters, reminding them all what they stood for.

King Tama sat beside sandwiched between his sons at the centre of the raised table, surveying everything as the local members took their seats.

As the gavel banged and the session began. Having made his own deals as the cabinet members drifted in, Aleki let his mind wander back to Stella and the mess he had made of things. He'd taken her interview as a sign and sent a dozen long stemmed lavender roses from the car but was well aware that they wouldn't even come close to making amends, if she accepted them at all.

Good luck to that poor delivery person.

A hissing noise broke through his thoughts and drew his attention to Manu, who gestured with his head towards the large oval gathering of tables before them.

"Any new business?" The Speaker enquired, peering around the room.

"Yes!" Aleki shot to his feet. "Yes, I have new business!"

Startled glances floated up from the floor. Royal family members rarely presented items themselves, but that was the least of Aleki's concerns today.

"Boy." Tama's voice was low enough to go undetected anywhere but the dais. "What do you think you're doing?"

Aleki ignored his father. "I would like to move that we use the recent publicity around my engagement to strengthen our ties with New Zealand. Now seems like an ideal time to start addressing some of the issues we have had between our countries and develop the Pacific Partnership scheme further to include them, perhaps extending towards Australia."

"That is what our ambassador does." One cabinet member offered drily, earning himself a glare.

"And our ambassador will continue to do so. However, I am thinking of a more intimate, informal delegation. One that can help usher in the Alternatives Pathways Initiative by helping us source teachers and tradespeople from Avali who have left the island, and recruiting them back to help develop skills in our young people here."

Some murmuring followed.

"I don't think it's necessary." King Tama's voice was firm with authority. "Let's move on."

Shrugging, the Speaker banged the gavel, but Aleki's voice rose above the thwack of wood-on-wood.

"I disagree."

A hush ballooned through the hall. All attention was on him. "I would like to discuss the possibility of filling the position myself."

His father snorted. "You?"

"Yes. I have more than proven myself in the last four years. I have been an excellent representative for our country."

"You have been a drunken moron!"

Aleki steeled himself. "I was. Once. I have not been that man for a long time now and anyone who still thinks that underestimates me. My recent work in securing the Samoan trade agreement should stand as evidence that I am capable of producing the results we need.

"Politics has a long memory, boy." The other cabinet members were openly watching the power struggle before them now.

"And I am prepared to make sure they remember me for all the right reasons."

"Not just for knocking up some *palagi* girl out of wedlock?"

All the air was sucked out of the room as the Avalian parliament collectively gasped.

Rage filled Aleki as he glared down at his father. "Hallway. Now." His voice was barely recognisable through gritted teeth.

"I don't think--"

"*Now.*"

The two of them stormed into the hallway, Manu following laconically. As soon as the assembly hall door shut behind them, Tama rounded on Aleki.

"How dare you undermine me in front of our people?"

"Me? How dare you talk down about the woman I love?"

"Love?" Tama scoffed. "What do you know of love?"

"I know enough to recognise it when it comes my way. I know enough to realise when I've messed it up." Aleki paused, levelling a hard look at his father. "I know that I didn't feel it enough growing up."

"Of course I love you," the king thundered. "Everything I do is for you!"

"Then why won't you let me do this?"

"Because she will ruin you!"

The words echoed through the high-ceilinged hallway, fading under the harsh saw of breath as father and son faced each other down.

Confusion sliced through Aleki's anger. "What?"

"That girl. Stella. She will ruin you." Tama's voice was quieter now. "I saw it when you came home from university. I saw it when you brought her to my home. You love her more than she loves you. It is a weakness."

"Father," Aleki placed a hand on his father's shoulder, noting the slight rounding, the hint of a slope that revealed the man's age. "Being in love is not a weakness. It is a gift."

"Pah," his father spat. "You sound like one of those head-shrinkers on television."

Aleki shrugged. "I have been talking to someone."

Tama's eyes narrowed. "Telling someone our family secrets? That is not the Avali way, boy. If you have a problem, you sort it out yourself. To ask for help is weakness. That is the white girl's influence on you."

"It is my choice." Aleki stood firm. "I do not feel weak for trying to understand myself better. Stella did not ask me to do this. Stella is still unlikely to speak to me ever again." Pain lanced his chest at the thought. "But I will be the best man I can be in case she does. And for our baby. Even if that means you no longer consider me an appropriate heir."

Tama nodded slowly. "And your decision is final? It is the woman or the title?"

"No. I want both. But if I must choose, it will be Stella

and our child. I can cope with not being a king. I cannot cope with not being a good man."

His father faltered and Aleki saw his chance. "I know how much you suffered when Mother died. The love you had for her, it shines out of the pictures. But I cannot stop loving Stella in case I lose her one day. Closing myself off from love does not make me strong. My strength comes from having her by my side. The way you had our mother."

Tama's eyes slid to Manu, who was lounging against a carved wooden fertility statue watching their exchange closely. "Are you happy to take his place?"

"Nope," Manu replied cheerfully. "I don't want to lead. I like to follow. I would make a poor ruler and we all know it. It's Aleki or nobody."

Another slow nod. "Then let us discuss how we shall proceed."

———

STELLA SUCKED down the last of her chocolate milk, hoping the benefits of the calcium for the baby would be enough to cancel out the sugar. It was her second of the morning - the stress of knowing her interview had aired in Avali several hours before she rose from her bed had led to a mass consumption of flavoured dairy goods. She'd drunk the first one while watching the interview itself on the Avali television network's app. She'd cracked the lid on the second as the office phone started ringing off the hook with requests from New Zealand magazines to cover her assumed heartbreak in full scorned-woman glory. Jessie had been forced to transfer calls to their out-of-office answering service. Still she'd heard nothing from the man she'd hoped would call. In a shocking moment of weakness, she'd even had Mae message him. No reply.

What did you expect? You left the damn country after a single fight. He probably feels relieved not to have to deal with your lunacy.

"Hey there, girlie."

Jesus Christ, cut me some slack.

She twisted in her chair just enough to send a withering look at the man standing in her doorway.

"Been awhile."

"Because you only show up when you run out of money." Stella turned back to her run sheet for the Chamber of Commerce awards dinner.

"Saw you on the news." Of course the national media had picked up on her piece with Tala.

"And now you see me in person. Hurrah."

"I'd like to see a bit more of you."

"Piss off, Graham."

"Like to see a bit more of my grandbaby too."

Blood rushed in her ears. "What the fuck did you just say?" Her voice sounded like it was being pulled through taffy, thick and slow.

"You're looking a little fuller there, girlie." Graham wandered into her eye-line, gesturing down at her breasts and torso. "Your mother was the same way. Green around the gills and popping out of her pants early on. You look like she did when she was carrying you. But you're my daughter through and through, aren't ya?" He settled in one of the plush blue chairs in front of her desk and Stella made a mental note to have it recovered immediately. "A prince, huh? Nice work if you can get it."

In and out. In and out. In and out.

"So let's talk visiting rights."

Laughter blurted from Stella's mouth like a foghorn. "I wouldn't let you near my child if the only other babysitting option was Jeffrey Dahmer."

"No time with the kid? Aw, that's a shame." Graham's mouth twisted in a sardonic grin. "I'm gonna miss that. How much do you reckon it's worth for me to leave the little sprout alone?"

There it is.

The shakedown wasn't a surprise, but Stella still felt it like a kick to the gut. *Of all the people a girl is supposed to be able to count on...*

She took another deep breath and a second to organise her thoughts before meeting her father's smug eyes.

"You listen to me, Graham Warren," she began, in the coldest voice she could muster, fixing him with the glare that had once caused an errant groomsman to literally crap his pants. Admittedly, he'd been deeply hungover. "I owe you nothing. You're a shitty human and a worse father. If it wasn't for Mum's memory I would have cut you loose at eighteen. And that's what I'm doing now. If you ever come near me or any member of my family again, if you try and make one red cent from my life, I will destroy you. I know all the bookies you cheated, I know all the scams you ran. I will give your name to every heavy in town and they will find you. I will have every speeding ticket and drunk driving incident and drug charge pulled out into the open and I will create such a fuss that any judge in this country will wet himself with excitement at the idea of being the one to do me a favour by putting you away. Hell, Luke will consider it a wedding gift to me. So, you get your filthy arse up off my chair and you walk out of this office right now on knees that I still allow to work, and you thank God that I am not a vengeful person. But if you ever cross me, if you give one interview, show up at one kindergarten session, try and buy my child a fucking ice-cream cone, know that I will find you and I will ruin every single part of your life until you are dead and cold in the ground."

Stella watched with a flat, frozen glower as the man who'd let her down every day of her life stood, shuffled uncomfortably on his feet, then left her office in silence, her eyes following him each step of the way. When she heard the main shop door close behind him, she leaned back and exhaled gustily, blowing out twenty-eight years of hopes and despair.

Finally, it's over.

Perhaps she should have felt a sense of mourning, but she'd been grieving the father she'd never had for as long as she could remember. The only thing left in her was an overwhelming relief that her child would never feel as unloved as she had. For all of Aleki's faults, he already loved their child unconditionally. It was in everything he had said and done since he'd discovered the existence of the precious life buried within her.

That thought warmed her, melting away any vestiges of the coldness she'd felt in Avali. She could see clearly now the pressure Aleki had been under, torn between his love for his country and his care for her and their child. Unlike Graham, all of Aleki's actions had been driven by his inherent goodness - wanting to please everyone. It wasn't his fault that her desperate need to feel like the most important thing had spilled over into the very real need for him to do the best for his people. How could she ask that her selfish desires outweigh the needs of an entire country?

Oh no. I've been such a fool.

Tears stung at the back of her eyes. She loved Aleki, the reality of that throbbed through her as true and as tangible as her own heartbeat. Yet when he needed her support and her understanding, she'd demanded his attention to try and heal the ugly scars of her past.

He'd been a better partner to her than she had to him.

Resolve strengthened her. She straightened her spine and blinked back her tears. Now was not the time to mope and feel sorry for herself. Now was the time for action.

"Stella?" A knock sounded at the door and Jessie stuck her head around the jamb. "Are you okay?"

Stella offered her assistant a tired smile.

"I'm okay."

Jessie said nothing, but raised an eyebrow and eyed Stella's midriff.

"Ugh." Stella sighed. "How did you know?"

"The exhaustion. The frequent toilet visits. The fact that I've never seen you eat a steak and cheese pie before, but you had one for lunch three times last week."

Stella wrinkled her nose. "I hate them. Why does my body want them so much?"

"So, about my job..."

"Yes, your job. I wanted to talk to you about that." Straightening, Stella motioned to the chairs in front of her desk and closed the binder for the Chamber of Commerce event. Her diminutive redheaded assistant sat perched on one like she was ready to take flight, teeth worrying at her bottom lip.

"Your job is safe, Jessie. We're booked right through the upcoming wedding season and have deposits down for at least half our available dates for the following season, as well as the corporate calendar events. Your coverage of client meetings and the admin side of things while I was in Avali was sensational. I don't want you to leave. In fact,"

Stella hesitated, trying to gauge Jessie's reaction. "I'd like to make you a partner in the business."

Colour bloomed in Jessie's cheeks.

"A partner?"

Stella hurried on. "I know you're young, but you've been working here since you finished school. You're an enthusiastic and personable assistant with strong attention to detail. You know our clients, our vendors and -- most importantly -- the level of quality Stella Warren Events aspires to. With the baby coming, I'm going to need to bring someone on, and I'd like to offer you the opportunity first."

"But, the money--".

"We can work out a payment structure for the initial buy-in and increasing stakeholder potential, if you're happy with that." She paused slightly. "There is one condition."

Jessie, still looking fairly stunned, nodded mutely.

As Stella laid out the details, hope bubbled deep inside her. She would make this right. For Aleki, for their baby, but most of all for herself. And maybe, if she was lucky, they could work together to build the beautiful future he'd hinted at, free from the resentment and expectations she'd burdened him with.

SEVENTEEN

The Wellington Chamber of Commerce dinner was lovely. Spread out across the ballroom of one of the finest hotels in the city, it was free of garish neon uplights and balloon arches. Instead, crystal chandeliers and warm candlelight spun prisms of light across a sea of crisp white tablecloths while tall plinths held flower arrangements in creams and yellows stationed evenly around the room.

As the event's MC made his closing remarks from the stage, he skirted around the edge of tables filled with business people high on the table wines and their own success, his eyes roaming over the crowd in search of one person.

He finally found her, clad in the black sequin dress from Mae and Luke's wedding, her stomach swelling slightly under the clingy fabric. The vision socked him in the gut, lust and love and longing all wrapped up in one thick fist that stopped him in his tracks. As he watched, she lowered her head to speak into her small headset, her eyes scanning the room. Even from the shadows her gaze poured over him like warm honey when they locked eyes. He moved towards her, measured steps that masked the wild thump of his heart until he stopped just out of arm's reach.

"Aleki." Stella sounded out of breath.

"Little star. I have missed you."

That was all it took. She threw herself into his arms, knocking her headset askew and he revelled in the warm press of her body, the crisp scent of her perfume, the rub of the silken strands along his jawline as he pressed kisses to her hair and forehead.

"I'm so sorry, Aleki. I'm sorry I didn't believe in you."

"Hush, little star. I gave you no reason to. I can never forgive myself for undermining your importance to me and I will spend every moment of the rest of our lives making it up to you, if you'll let me." Pulling back, he stared down into her shining green eyes. "I love you, Stella Warren. I love you for your strength, your righteousness, your good heart, your clever brain, and everything in between. I love you for giving me the blessing of a child and for giving me yourself without reservations. I am so sorry I could not do the same for you from our beginning. Can you ever forgive me for being too scared to see that what we have is stronger than any of my fears?"

"Of course," she whispered, pressing her palm against his cheek. "Of course I can. I love you so much, Aleki. I'm so sorry I left."

"No, my star, you were right to go. You knew you deserved better than I was giving you."

The music swelled in the background as the band started playing. Tiki Taane's 'Always On My Mind'. The hundred dollars he'd flicked the guitarist on his way into the venue had been worth it.

"Will you dance with me, my love?"

"God, yes."

He led her onto the dancefloor, the thrum of the reggae-based beat washing over him as he finally held the woman he loved in his arms, free of the fear that had dogged him the entirety of his adult life.

"Aleki?" Stella blinked up at him, her eyes huge and lovely under the sparkling lights. "I have something to tell you. I'm taking on a new partner. Jessie is buying into the business. I'm going to be able to do a lot more work remotely, even--" she hesitated slightly "--even from over-seas. For at least six months of the year I can live fully in Avali, and then just come back every three to four weeks for the wedding season."

His body stopped swaying and he clutched her to him tighter. "Are you serious? You did that? For me?"

"For us." Stella corrected, firmly. "I want us to be a family. We can't be a family from three thousand kilometres away. Our baby needs their father there for school plays and sports games and scraped knees and to learn about their country and culture."

"Oh my love," he sighed into her hair. "My love. You didn't have to do that."

"I wanted to. It's time to give up a little control. Our child isn't the only one who needs to feel loved, Aleki. You need to feel it too, and that means I need to be there to make sure you do."

Cradling her face in his hands, Aleki pressed a kiss to her lips, surrendering to their sweetness. Lifting his head, he gazed into her eyes.

"I've discussed my role with my father. For the next ten years while he's still able to rule, my royal duties will be reduced. We're forming several Parliamentary subcommit-tees to cover some of my former roles, and I've been assigned an ambassador-like role to New Zealand with the sole focus of strengthening relationships between our countries. I was planning on moving here fulltime. If you're happy to move to Avali, I'll be able to travel with you and the baby when you come back as part of that official role."

"Oh!" Stella sighed up at him, her eyes shining with love. "You would sacrifice the time with your people for our family?"

A growl rumbled out of his throat. "I would do anything for you, little star. You are the light of my life, and I will spend every day of our lives proving it to you."

"Yeah?" Stella pressed the lush curves of her body against him, a playful smirk pulling at her lips. "And what about the nights? Will you spend any of the nights proving it to me?"

His blood heated, swirling down and pulling tight through his groin. "I'll prove it to you tonight."

Desire swam in Stella's gaze. Without breaking eye contact, she pulled at the headset looped around her neck and spoke into the mouthpiece.

"Jessie? Meet me at the ballroom entrance. It's time for you to take the reins."

Her delighted laughter floated behind him as he pulled her off the floor and practically dragged her towards the entrance, their fingers linked tightly. After a breathless handover to Jessie, Aleki led his woman to the elevator bank and stabbed at the button for the penthouse.

"You have a room?"

"I do," he growled, watching the climbing numbers light up the screen.

"That seems presumptuous."

"Not presumptuous, my love. Desperate, yes. And perhaps optimistic. You have given me the courage to take chances, and this one has paid off."

She melted into him as soon as the doors closed behind them, their lips locking as he ran his hands down her body, grasping at the lush curves of her ass.

The bell dinged and they stumbled out of the elevator into the penthouse suite, zips and buttons loosening at the speed of light. Finally they tumbled on the bed, skin-to-skin, as he gazed down at her, caramel waves spread across crisp white cotton, like a shining angel that had saved him from his lonely life. Then she moved, sliding one perfect leg up over his hip and he was lost. He plunged into her, eyes rolling back into his head at the warm, perfect fit of her body around his, holding him a prisoner of lust as his body rejoiced in the feeling of coming home. After several long moments he felt her flex around him and he moved, long, slow unhurried drags designed to tease and worship while sensation buzzed at the base of his spine. When Stella's breath came in sharp, hot pants, he reached down and pressed against the tight bundle of nerves, his lips never leaving her skin, kissing and licking and whispering promises onto the surface of her body where they settled like tattoos. Then she was clenching around him in waves, gripping at the base of him in a perfect clutch of heat while she gasped words of love that flowed over his skin and down his torso, wrapping around him and carrying him over the edge on a tidal wave of desire.

Satisfaction settled over him, a thick golden blanket that wrapped around his body as he pressed a lingering kiss to the lips of his beloved and stroked his hand across the light swell of her stomach where their baby grew.

This is where you belong. This is home.

EPILOGUE

"I swear to God, if you keep dragging me through the bush in this dress, I'll never blow you again."

Aleki's laugh bounced off the surrounding native plants as he guided Stella down the rocky steps. She held his hands tightly, the darkness from the blindfold he'd slipped over her eyes before entering the car disorientating her.

She took small steps, glad she'd heeded his suggestion to wear flats. The golden sandals wouldn't normally be her first choice with her cream silk slip dress, but between the blindfold and the swell of her five-month pregnant stomach she was grateful to avoid any balance issues heels might have caused.

"We're here." Her fiancé's voice rumbled in her ear, as he slid one hand around her hip and quickly patted the bump where their baby grew. Since they'd announced the pregnancy, he'd taken every opportunity to touch and caress the changing landscape of her body, leaving her in no doubt of his desire for her and for his upcoming role as a father.

She'd been lucky that the lawyers had managed to work out the partnership terms with Jessie so quickly. The newly rebranded Star and Steel Event Management Agency had shown no signs of slowing down. In fact Stella's remote workdays were as full now as they'd ever been, even with Jessie on-site for facilities and meetings in Wellington.

Stella stood still as Aleki gently removed the blindfold from her eyes, but gasped at the sight revealed before her. The Grotto shimmered with light, like a golden cave from an animated film. Long tables were laid with low vases of lavender roses and thousands of string lights adorned the railing that separated the cliffside from the ocean below. At one end of the restaurant an archway adorned with monstera leaves, white gardenias and orchids rose towards the stalactite ceiling. To her left, Jessie, Sio and Oliana, Lani and her girlfriend Pania, Mae and Luke, Andreas, Manu and King Tama stood gathered in a small huddle, dressed in both Western and Pacific formalwear.

Aleki cleared his throat, and captured her attention as he stood slightly stiffly in front of her. At some point in the car journey he must have changed from her favourite olive tshirt into a floaty white linen shirt and a frangipani lei.

"Stella Rose Warren," he began, his dark eyes boring into her. "I love you and I always will. I know you said you didn't mind waiting until after our *pepe* arrives, but I want our child to know that it's parents were as committed as two people could be before he or she makes its way into this world. Will you do me the honour, now, in front of our friends and family, of becoming my wife?"

Moisture built behind Stella's eyes and she blinked rapidly to stop the fall of her tears of joy.

"Yes," she blurted. "Of course I will."

Relief lit Aleki's face and he squeezed her hands together in his. Stepping closer as their guests busied themselves moving closer to the arch, he lowered his forehead to hers and inhaled deeply.

"I can't wait to meet our baby as husband and wife."

Stella smiled, the knowledge swelling in her and spilling out of her mouth. "You think she'll be happy to see us?"

Aleki's eyes flew open and he pulled back slightly to meet her gaze. "She?"

Stella nodded, and joy spread across his face. "She," he repeated in wonder. "I hope she's just like her mother. I'd be the luckiest man alive."

Stella beamed, elated. "We're lucky to have you. Shall we

make this thing official then?"

Bright white teeth flashed at her. "Let's go."

Fingers linked, she walked into the restaurant with her prince.

Into our future.

THE END.

Read on for an excerpt of *Crown Chemistry*, Manu's Story

"But I hate people." Clare Trescott's voice echoed through her living room - her lovely, empty living room - like the bells of war.

"I know you do." The smooth tones of Theo 'Tex' Miller, her former foster brother, current landlord and only true friend, hummed through her phone speaker. "Think of it as a favour to me."

"Letting some random sleep in your bedroom for three months while you're off saving the world is a favour to you?"

"Not technically a random," Tex offered, holding it out like a consolation prize over the phone. "A friend of a friend of a friend. Apparently, the place he was supposed to be in fell through. And to be honest—" he hesitated briefly, "—I already said yes. He's supposed to be there around eight tonight. I could use the rent money, Clare."

Clare pulled a face at the phone, secure in the knowledge that Tex was a zillion miles away in some unknown foreign land, doing God-knows-what for the New Zealand Army, while she sat wrapped up in three blankets on his tan leather sectional.

"Fine." She sighed into the phone. The money factor was one she couldn't argue with. Growing up in the system together, both she and Tex had a burning need for financial security. He'd used his military money to put a deposit on the Auckland city flat they shared, and he'd cut her a deal on rent while she'd studied fertility science. Now that she'd worked her way up to be an embryologist in a private clinic in the city she paid her fair share, but she always felt slightly indebted to Tex for the support he'd given her in the early years. "I'll let a stranger move in here. Short term *only*." She stressed the last word, concern that Tex might pull this crap every time he was stationed overseas creeping in.

"And you'll be nice?"

"I'm always nice."

A snort echoed down the phone, matching her own as they sniggered together over her blatant lie.

"I'll be as nice as I can," Clare amended, as she fiddled with the silver St Christopher's necklace Tex had given her for her twenty-first birthday.

"I appreciate it, Clare Bear. You're the best."

"No, you are." She sighed down the phone again. "I'll talk to you later. Stay safe."

"You too, Clare Bear. Nighty night."

Clare thumbed off her phone and tossed it further down the couch, before exhaling heavily as she glanced around the open-plan kitchen and living area. She loved this apartment - like *love, loved* it - and the idea of sharing her personal space for the first time in a decade with anyone who wasn't Tex niggled at her like a thorn in her side.

Eighteen years in the foster care system had bred a natural wariness into her. Having never been adopted, she'd come across all sorts in her journey - she'd been burgled, spat on and verbally abused by both the parents and kids who'd claimed to want to care for her over the years. That was why Tex's small two-bedroom flat, with its big caramel couch, plain white walls and bulbous hanging copper light shades, felt like such a haven. She never had to worry when she was here. Bringing someone else into their sanctuary was a risk she wouldn't have taken voluntarily, but it wasn't her call. If Tex said he needed rent money, then he needed it. And she would never deny Tex something he needed.

Clare checked her watch. *Seven pm. Plenty of time for dinner.* She hefted a chunky cream blanket off her and stood, stretching towards the ceiling as high as her five-foot four frame could reach, and then sank forward into a toe-touch. Energy zinged through her legs and up her torso as the muscles lengthened. Straightening, she headed down the hall to the apartment entrance and grabbed her cheery yellow coat off the hook by the door and her e-reader off the table under it. Skipping the lift, she bounced down five flights of stairs, out the glass doors and into the pub on the corner.

"Hey, Clare," Cole the Bartender greeted her. "The usual?"

"The usual." She headed to the back booth, empty as it always was on a Tuesday night, chucked her coat onto the burgundy velour and slid in beside it, powering on her e-reader.

Bliss.

Tuesdays at the pub were her ritual. A steak meal and raspberry fizzy drink, with a few chapters to read while she waited. No phone, no distractions, just satisfying food for her belly and her brain. Tuesdays were the only weeknight she didn't stay at work past five reading up on conception rates and genome testing. The world of fertility science was fast-paced, and if she wanted a promotion to Laboratory Manager, she needed to keep on top of any rapid developments that could be useful in the New Zealand market.

Tex joined her for her weekly meal when he was in town, and over the last few years, she'd become enough of a regular that she'd seen Cole the Bartender go from a skinny kid fresh from high school to a married man with a child of his own.

She'd just gotten comfortable when there was a thunk

and a literal god sat down across from her in the booth, grinning at her over a pint of amber beer.

"Hey there."

Clare stared at him, positive the horror coursing through her system was readable on her face. Not only was he *in her Tuesday booth*, but he was quite possibly the most attractive man she'd ever laid eyes on.

Warm brown eyes, crinkled at the corner like they were sharing a joke, danced out at her from the dark skin of his face. His features were all large - a wide nose and full lips framed by a strong jaw and high forehead. A single dimple creased his left cheek. His long hair was pulled back from his face and lay in two tidy braids across shoulders that looked like they could be used for transporting a busload of small children to safety in the event of a flood. Not unlike the sudden one in her pants.

Still smiling at her, he cocked an eyebrow. Awareness that she was staring like a moron drifted through her, slow at first, then speeding up until the hot flush of embarrassment slid up her neck.

"Can I help you?"

"I'm killing time until an appointment. Do you mind if I sit here?"

"Yes," Clare replied bluntly, but the Stranger God just laughed and nodded towards her e-reader.

"What are you reading about?"

"Venereal diseases." It was true. She was reading the biography of Ettie Rout, a New Zealand nurse famous for working to protect soldiers from sexually transmitted diseases during World War One.

The Stranger God's thick eyebrows shot up.

"Do you have one?"

"Go away."

He laughed again, a deep, rich sound with the hint of an accent that reached inside her and twisted. She shook her head as though she could mentally bat away the glow in her chest at his attention and refocused on her screen.

A beat. Then ...

"I'm thinking about getting one of those. Do you reckon they're better than actual books?"

Clare sighed heavily. First, Tex letting a stranger move into the apartment, and now this. Was there no end to her torment today? Very deliberately, she powered off the device, flipped the cover closed and placed it on the polished wood of the table. She raised her eyes to the Stranger God's, ignoring the frisson of awareness that ran straight from her nipples to her underwear, and enunciated clearly.

"What. Do. You. Want?"

"I'd like to take you out sometime. If that's not an option, I'd like to chat to you now while I wait."

"No."

"No?"

"You heard me." She narrowed her eyes, pinning him with Death Glare Number Two. "I'm here alone, and I don't want company. In a minute, I'm going to eat the best steak in the central city, finish a single chapter of my book, then go home and put on flannel pyjamas. This is my only night off. I have no desire to sit here stroking your ego while you hope you're charming enough to talk me into stroking something else. It's not going to happen. Please leave me alone."

His surprised gaze roamed over her face, and for a second she thought she was going to have to upgrade to Death Glare Number Three, but he nodded and slid out of the booth.

"I'm sorry to have disturbed you, miss. My apologies. Please enjoy your evening."

He gave a funny little bow motion and wandered back towards the bar just as Cole the Bartender rounded it with her meal and walked over to set the plate in front of her.

She did a happy little dance in her seat at the sight of the juicy steak piled high atop a stack of thick, golden chips and the side salad peeking around from the back. Still, even as she sank her knife through beef that parted like butter, a feeling of being watched niggled at the base of her spine. It lingered throughout her meal, seasoning the flavour of the food, but every time she snuck a look at the bar, where the only other patron sat, the Stranger God and Cole the Bartender were engaged in a lively debate about some kind of sportsball being shown on the telly above the rows of gleaming bottles.

When frustration over her inability to concentrate on her book finally edged out the stubbornness that had kept her trying for a full half hour after she'd cleaned her plate, she stood. Shoving her fists through the arms of her yellow coat, she headed towards the bar, where Cole the Bartender now leaned alone, despite the inexplicable presence of a suitcase by the register.

"All done?"

"All done." She fished in her coat pocket for her card, but he shook his head.

"No need. Your mate took care of it."

Shock coursed through Clare. "The human mountain paid for my dinner?"

"That's the one."

"But ..." She floundered. "I don't want him to."

"Too late. You can go wait for him outside the toilets if you want to argue with him about it. But Amanda keeps reminding me that the world is hard enough for women. Take your free meals where you can get them."

"There's no such thing as a free meal," Clare intoned darkly, her brows pulling together.

"Well, you and my lovely wife can debate that point in your own time. For now, your tab is clear."

"But—"

"Clare." He interrupted with exaggerated patience. "Do you have any idea how much that man makes?"

Confusion tripped through her. What had Cole done? Run a credit check on his customer? Did the Stranger God have one of those fancy bank cards with 'Esquire' stamped on it? She hadn't taken him for the sort who cared about a person's wealth.

"No?"

Cole the Bartender laughed. "Trust me. Your steak isn't going to make a dent. Will I see you tomorrow?"

Clare snorted in response. He'd been trying to get her to the pub on Wednesdays for the best part of two years.

"Not a chance, Cole the Bartender. See you next week."

ACKNOWLEDGMENTS

My heartfelt thanks go out to Barbara De Leo and Hayson Manning for their ongoing feedback, encouragement and advice. I am so lucky to have their expertise to draw on. The deepest thanks to the Blenheim girls for bringing me into the fold as a newbie with a decent first chapter.

From the bottom of my heart I would like to thank the Pacific Islanders who have spent the last decade educating me in their languages and cultures, answering my questions and sharing their experiences, and to Vika Mana for her work in ensuring cultural elements of this book were handled as sensitively as possible. Any mistakes are mine alone.

No book is born without suffering and I have not suffered alone. I cannot give enough thanks to my husband for the support and encouragement he has given me in this journey, even though he explicitly said 'Don't thank me, I don't need acknowledgement'. My unending appreciation also extends to my parents and the Disney+ app, both of whom did a little more babysitting than I'd like to admit to during this process.

ABOUT THE AUTHOR

Award-winning author Courtney Clark Michaels has been reading and writing romance since she first pilfered a novel out of her mother's bedroom at the tender age of thirteen. Courtney's passion for writing strong, independent heroines and smart, sexy men is equal only to her passions for travel, online shopping and patting other people's dogs. She is lucky enough to live in the heart of New Zealand's wine-making region with her opposites-attract hero, a few gorgeous children and a hyperactive poochon named Kevin.

ALSO BY COURTNEY CLARK MICHAELS

PACIFIC PASSIONS

Crown Chemistry

Heiress Undone

Christmas in Paradise

Ginger Kisses

Counting Down

Storm Warning

HOT RUGBY KNIGHTS

Game Changer

Off His Game

STANDALONES

Single Dad For The Runaway Bride

Royally Screwed

A Pacific Passions story

By Courtney Clark Michaels

This book is a work of fiction. Names, characters, places and incidents are the product of the author's imagination or are used fictitiously. Any resemblance to persons living or dead is coincidental.

Previously published as *Pregnant By The Prince*.

Cover Illustration - Kerilyn Clarke

Ebook ISBN: 978-1-0670246-5-9

Print ISBN: 978-1-0670246-6-6